NO GOOD PLAYS

A Q.C. DAVIS MYSTERY NOVELLA

LISA M. LILLY

SPINY WOMAN LLC

1

"You're asking me to look into this death?" I said. "Or find out about your son's life and report to you? Because if it's the second one, I don't owe you that many favors."

Detective Sergeant Beckwell and I sat outside the Starbucks at the corner of Michigan Avenue and Jackson. The wind shifted, whipping my long hair into my face and raising goosebumps on my bare shoulders though it was early July. I slipped my blazer back on, glad I'd grabbed it on my way of the office. The sound of rhythmic drumming came from across the street where a row of five kids played white plastic tubs turned upside down and into makeshift drums. Visitors to Chicago's Art Institute lingered on its concrete steps, watching and listening.

"No reporting." Detective Beckwell ran his hand over his salt-and-pepper hair. His crewcut and perfectly straight posture gave him an ex-military look, but his slightly too large tan suit always made me think of an old-fashioned private eye. "But as you try to figure out the coach's death, if you learn anything that can help Josh all the better."

"But how would I explain being at the high school? I'm guessing Catholic schools – all schools – frown on random people coming in to ask questions."

"My ex-wife's on the board. The school has a three-week intensive summer theater program. They perform some sort of play the students wrote during spring semester. She says they'd love someone like you to help."

"It's a long time since I acted professionally," I said.

As a child, I worked a fair amount in storefront theaters, and some larger ones, in the Chicago area. But my last paid acting job was in college. Now I'm a lawyer. I draw on some of the skills I learned in theater, though not necessarily the ones people expect. Those skills had also helped me find out the truth about crimes that puzzled the police. Or, more accurately, that didn't come to their attention. Beckwell and I crossed paths because of that more than once. The first time had been when I lost someone I loved.

Beckwell leaned forward, resting crossed arms on the metal table and making it wobble. "Quille, the head of the drama department, if you can call it that, is an English lit teacher who acted in a few community theater shows decades ago. I guarantee you did more professional acting by the time you were twelve than she has in her whole life."

"Don't knock community theater. I've seen some pretty amazing productions." I sipped the Chai latte Beckwell had bought for me. It was finally cool enough to drink. "But how does helping with summer theater get me near the basketball team? Or your son?"

"The volunteer badge gets you into all school activities. You're resourceful. If nothing else, you can go to the basketball practices. They start at seven at night. That's after the play rehearsals finish. Watch. Get to know some of the team. Maybe Josh."

"They practice in the summer?"

"Technically it's open gym. But all the team members go."

Across the street, the kids finished with a last bang and twirled their drumsticks in unison. Onlookers clapped. Some dropped coins and bills in the upright plastic bucket in front of the drummers.

"Detective –"

He held up his hand. "Wayne."

It was the first time he'd suggested I call him by his first name. Probably because, for once, I wasn't doing what he saw as interfering in police business.

"Wayne, I'm sorry your son is struggling. But I'm a solo lawyer. If I'm not working, I make zero. Nothing. And, oddly enough, all my bills still come due at the end of the month."

"I'm not asking you to quit your law practice." Beckwell spread his hands, nearly knocking over his coffee. He moved it toward the center of the table. "Just volunteer in the afternoons for three weeks. You've done this kind of thing before. Marco's son, your friend at the café, that loser you went to grade school with. "

"Those had special circumstances. Reasons my insights made a difference. This – you could hire a private investigator. Or do it yourself."

He frowned. "No jurisdiction. And my superiors won't want me messing in Riverside's investigation – whether I do it or I hire someone."

That explained the meeting at Starbucks. Before tonight, the only place I ever saw Detective Sergeant Beckwell was at a crime scene or at his office at Chicago's 18th and State Street police station.

"Don't you think they'll trace my involvement back to you if it comes down to it?"

"So? You're a family friend with relevant theater experience. I asked you to volunteer and look in on my son, maybe help find out what's troubling him. If you stumble onto some answers about the coach's death, that's just how it happened."

I raised my eyebrows. "Stumbling? That's the way you see me?"

"Obviously this is me admitting it's a lot more than that. But it's a plausible story for the powers that be if I need it. And you don't need to figure out everything. Just enough to find a likely suspect. There was DNA other than the coach's at the scene and on his body, but it didn't match anything in any database. If you can show someone's a legitimate suspect, or more than one person, the police can get DNA samples, see if there's a match."

"You make it sound so easy."

"I know it's not. C'mon, Quille. I'll owe you."

Which was the real reason I was here. A Detective Sergeant with the Chicago PD was a good friend to have. That and I felt for him over his worries about his son. I don't have kids myself, but I'm close with my niece and nephew. And with the teenage son of the man I'd been seeing two years ago, the one whose death caused Beckwell and me to meet.

"And how do you think the coach's death connects with your son?"

"Feel it in my gut." He patted his mid-section which, for a man in his late fifties, still looked pretty flat. "Old cop's intuition. A couple weeks before the coach's death I saw changes in Josh. Always exhausted. Snapped at me no matter what I said. My ex told me he'd been having trouble sleeping for months. Moody. This spring the team won a few games in the state tournament. Never happened before. And he wasn't excited about it. Didn't want me to come to the pep rally celebrating it. Which made no sense because he's the captain, and it's the first winning year the basketball team ever had."

"But why connect it to the coach?"

"Because Coach Taylor started last fall. Hired to whip the team into shape, and he did. Then he gets mugged, supposedly, in the faculty parking lot. After the pep rally to celebrate his season."

"The rally your son didn't want you to come to."

"That's the one."

I didn't want to ask the next question. But I had to. "Are you afraid Josh was involved somehow? Or knows something?"

Beckwell shook his head. "I don't for a second believe he did anything criminal. And, I know, parents whose kids have a rap sheet a mile long say that. But I know my son."

"And yet you're worried."

"He could know something and not realize it. Maybe about why it happened."

"Or who did it? He could be covering for someone."

"No. He'd tell me."

I felt less sure of that. If Josh suspected a friend was involved, for instance, he might protect that person, and it might weigh on him. But with the changes in him starting before the coach's death, that scenario seemed less likely.

"If Josh did something wrong," I said. "I don't

want to be in a position where I feel like I need to report it and you're telling me not to."

"My goal is to help him deal with whatever's happening, not cover anything up. But I'm not worried he's done something criminal. Just that he got in the middle of something."

Those things weren't mutually exclusive, but Beckwell already knew that.

I glanced sideways at a police SUV gliding to a stop in front of the hotel next door, blue lights flashing but sirens silent. No one got out.

"The Riverside police department must have investigated," I said. "I can't see why you need me."

The high school Josh attended, St. Angelina's, stood on the east edge of Riverside, a small suburb about nine miles west of downtown Chicago. It was on the same train line I took to LaGrange, the suburb where I grew up and my Gram still lived.

"Riverside has less than 10,000 people with next to zero violent crime," Beckwell said. "Their expertise is enforcing the village's draconian parking laws. Which they're excellent at, so watch where you park. But when it comes to murder, they might have missed a thing or two. Or a hundred."

I drank more of the latte, barely registering the spicy, creamy taste. In the last month I'd finally caught up with my law practice after spending too much time investigating an old friend's fears about his employer's untimely death. Not only had my friend, who hadn't like what I learned, not thanked me, I couldn't truly call him a friend anymore.

Also, I had been attacked, and I'd promised my friends and my Gram to act more cautiously in the future.

I set my drained cup on the table. "I wasn't planning on investigating any other crimes."

Beckwell smiled for the first time since we'd sat down. "Sure you weren't. And I'm going to retire next year."

2

OTHER THAN THE crucifix hanging on the wall behind her desk, the office of Apolonia Cieslak, who told me to call her Polly, looked much like what I guessed any other high school teacher's might. According to St. Angelina's website, Polly had a Bachelor of Arts Degree from Dominican University, but she wasn't a nun.

Still, the stern look she gave me called to mind all the stereotypes.

"Your experience is outdated." Polly shifted her clunky plastic keyboard to the side of her desk. Her black frame glasses and dark gray top and pants contrasted her silver-gray hair and gave her an artsy yet somewhat conservative look. "But it's more professional theater work than I ever did, since I did none. So there's that."

"You don't sound happy I'm here," I said.

The principal, after making sure I had signed all the forms he'd emailed to me the day before, had given me my volunteer badge and assured me the school was eager for all the help it could get. But maybe no one asked Polly what she wanted.

She studied her bulky computer monitor, which I assumed showed my resume. "Undergraduate business major, accounting work, then law school. You didn't consider theater as a major?"

At thirty-four, I hadn't expected to revisit my college major. "I minored in it. But my Gram suggested majoring in business and accounting if I meant to earn my living as an actor. And I found out I liked it. The business world. Most of my clients are small corporations or solo business owners. Though I represent some actors, too."

All of that was a vast oversimplification, but my difficult family history and how it affected my choices wasn't her business.

Polly took off her glasses, folded them, and tapped them against her open palm. "It just seems odd. I know more people who feel stuck in the corporate world. Frustrated they never followed their creativity."

"I still do creative things. For fun. But for work, I like law. And numbers. They add up or don't. You know where you stand."

When I mentioned numbers adding up, Polly stopped tapping her glasses. Her eyes narrowed. "I imagine law's not that clear cut."

"No, but it's a little like solving puzzles. Figuring out how the facts fit and what cases ought to apply."

The area around Polly's lips, which were pressed together, whitened. "Hm." She stood. "Well, you're here, and we're putting on a play in three weeks, so I can't say I can't use you."

The double negative and lack of enthusiasm combined left me feeling both less than welcome and curious what she might be worried I'd learn. I stood, too.

"Rehearsal's in the auditorium," Polly said. "The play's student written. By a group of kids from my junior Honors English class. You can observe our warm ups to start. Then there's table read. Did Scott send you a copy of the play?"

Scott Galleti was the principal, and he hadn't.

Polly sighed when I told her that and handed me a sheaf of pages from the corner of her desk.

Her heavy wood office door creaked when she opened it, and swung shut with a bang behind us. Polly locked it with a key, something the principal hadn't done with his office. Though he had an assistant to guard his door.

I followed her down the school's narrow hallways. They smelled of fresh pine. The floors were worn but shone in the fluorescent lighting. I was trying to think of a reason to ask about Coach Taylor when we turned a corner. Trophy cases lined one side of the hall.

"I heard about the basketball coach's death," I said. "It must've been a huge shock. Are the students handling it all right?"

Polly didn't slow her steps or glance at me as I half-expected at the mention of the sudden death. Maybe over the last two months she'd become used to questions. "It was shocking. But the counseling staff went into high gear. A neighboring Catholic school offered their staff, too. To help with grief counseling. Hardly any of my students knew him, though."

"In a school of nine hundred? I'd think all the students would know nearly every teacher."

This observation wasn't mine. I had done

self-study for high school, and nine hundred sounded large compared to writing essays at the dining room table or reading alone in my room. But my friend Lauren had attended a Catholic high school with about a thousand students. She claimed she knew every teacher there.

Polly stopped at a curved wall with double doors. "They know who he is. But he'd only been here a year. Only the students who had him for gym class or were on teams really interacted with him."

I followed her into the auditorium. It had graded seating and a balcony and smelled of dust and chalk. Faded, once-red velvet curtains had been drawn apart to reveal rows of risers upstage.

For most of the rehearsal I observed, though I suggested a few warm ups they hadn't tried before. During the table read I helped a few student actors struggling with lines. For a student-written production it wasn't bad, though from scene to scene the style changed. One student writer loved short, crisp sentences. Another must have been a literature major. The lines included more multiple syllable words than I saw in most legal briefs.

One girl, Rima, had a wide face and dark eyebrows that slashed down toward her nose. She asked a lot of questions about her character's motivation and made lots of notes in her script. I helped her through some of the more challenging lines, suggesting ways to break them into parts to make them easier to memorize.

When the class ended, rather than try to talk more with Polly, I followed Rima out the side door. A student's insights might tell me a lot more about the school than any teacher could.

"You've got a great start on your role," I said, which was true.

Rima's face lit. "You think? I wanted the lead but, you know, now I kind of like this character."

"I think she's more interesting because she's more complex. Wider range of emotions for you to play. Which is great experience if you're thinking of acting in college. Or beyond."

"Did you really work as a stage actress?"

"For a lot of years."

We'd reached the doors to outside. After two hours in the windowless auditorium, exiting to the school's front lawn felt like emerging from a darkened movie theater. I blinked as the sun hit my eyes and the warm, humid air surged over me.

"Is it – I know it's hard work. But did you like it? What was your favorite role?"

We sat on the concrete steps and I told her about a few productions and answered her other questions as she waited for her ride home. Like a lot of students, she lived a few suburbs away. Too far to walk, and the suburban public transportation system isn't as useful as the city's.

"Do you know Josh Beckwell?" I asked during a lull in the conversation. "His dad's a friend of mine."

"Everyone knows Josh," Rima said. "Captain of the basketball team. Cute. And nice. At least he used to be." She flushed.

"Used to be?"

"I just meant – forget it."

"I won't tell him anything you say. I know his dad, not him."

She stared at the sidewalk where a few shoots of green had burst through a crack. "Makes no diff. He doesn't know who I am, I'm sure."

"But you noticed he changed?"

"They all changed. When the team started winning. At first I was happy. Everyone was. I mean, even if you're not into sports, most people, it's kind of awesome to see a team that always lost get to win. You know?"

"But?"

She shrugged. "Went to their heads. I mean,

before they used to ignore us. No jocks in theater, you know. I heard Mrs. Cieslak arguing with Coach Taylor about it last fall."

It took me a second to realize she meant Polly Cieslak. I'd forgotten the last name, but of course the students didn't call her Polly.

"Arguing about no athletes in the theater department?"

"Yeah, I think that was it. I only heard the end of it. He said something like, 'my team, my players' and stomped off. He had a basketball with him. He, like, always carried one."

"So the team used to stay away from theater?"

"Still do. But now, well, doesn't matter now because it's summer. But all spring they bullied us. Wouldn't let us sit at our table in the cafeteria. So, fine, we pick a different table and next day they put backpacks and things all over that one. Didn't sit there, just got in our way. But when I moved their stuff, I got detention. Teachers never listen. All they asked was did I move other people's things."

"Unfair," I said.

"Yeah and my best friend's little sister, she was a freshman. They said she was too fat to be in the cafeteria. Started making pig noises, grunting and oinking, whenever she was in the food line or at a vending machine."

Whenever I hear people's high school stories, I can't help wondering how I would have felt if I went. This one made me glad I missed the experience. One director was awful to me when I went through a skinny, gawky phase with my dark, curly hair springing out everywhere and feeling like I didn't know what to do with my arms and legs. But he likely had been nothing compared to a bunch of teenagers.

"No one stopped them?" I said.

"The monitor told the coach and he yelled at them. But no detentions. I heard they did a couple extra sprints at practice. After that they only oinked at lunch if no teachers were around. But they did it during every passing period. Hung out in the main hall watching for her. Next year she's going to public school."

"And Josh took part in that?"

Rima frowned. "Not that I saw. But he always hangs with the team, and he didn't stop them. Then the guy who started it, he got cut from the team. And they made fun of him, too. Called him Drooler."

I couldn't puzzle out what that meant. "Meaning?"

She shrugged. "Dunno, but it makes him go all red in the face. Good on him. But didn't run him out of the school."

I wanted to ask her the friend's name and about Coach Taylor's death. But a small blue SUV pulled to the curb and honked. Rima thanked me for the acting tips again and headed across the lawn.

Open gym started at seven p.m., which left me nearly two hours to kill.

St. Angelina's stands on the edge of Riverside, but only a few blocks from its downtown area. The small suburb features winding streets, brick sidewalks, historic buildings, and a train station. At a sandwich shop near the train station I got a prosciutto and fresh mozzarella sandwich. I settled at a white wood table on the patio to eat and do a little work. On my phone, I reviewed a motion and sent a few changes to my paralegal to make overnight. She lives in another state and works remotely, often nights and weekends. Which meant I'd have everything back to me when I got to my office at eight a.m.

Finished with that, I called Beckwell's ex-wife, Nadine.

She answered right away. "Quille?"

"Yes, hello." We hadn't talked before, so Beckwell must have given her my cell phone number. I asked if she could fill in some blanks for me about the coach's death.

But she said, "Ask Wayne. He's the one who got you involved."

3

I scooted my chair sideways to get a better view of the park that ran alongside the river. "I got the impression you were on board with all this. Concerned about Josh."

"Of course I'm concerned about my son."

I pressed my fingers to my forehead. Usually I'm pretty good at diplomacy. But I hadn't expected hostility. "I only meant that you got me the volunteer position, so I thought you were on the same page as Wayne."

A sigh came through the phone. "We haven't been on the same page for a long time. But that's not your fault. I shouldn't have snapped at you."

I wondered briefly if she thought I was seeing Beckwell and that was the issue. I hadn't thought to ask how long they'd been divorced or when she remarried.

"So you don't think it's worth looking into the coach's death?"

"I'm concerned about Josh, and it's awful the coach got killed. But Wayne's seeing problems that aren't there. The police know what happened."

"You believe it was a mugging that got out of hand?" I said.

"What else? My husband says that faculty lot was the perfect set up for it, and I agree."

"Beckwell – Wayne – said his cop instincts told him otherwise."

"My husband's a cop too. Forest Park."

Beckwell had failed to mention that. I wondered if I'd gotten in the middle of some weird rivalry between the two men.

"Why is the faculty lot a perfect set up?"

"Have you seen it?" Nadine said.

"I parked there today."

Tomorrow I planned to take the train here from downtown. But knowing I'd be at the open gym tonight, I'd driven.

"Well it wasn't like that before. Anyone could go in. The gate, the fencing, the security cameras. None of that was there. Talk about spending on barn doors only after the horses escape."

"Budget issues?"

"Always."

The wood and metal desks I'd seen in the principal's and Polly's offices and their outdated computer equipment confirmed that. Though I wasn't sure why. The yearly tuition matched what I paid for law school.

"Still, you can't see the faculty lot, or the student lot, from the main streets," I said.

St. Angelina's stood on a corner. Busy four-lane streets bordered its east and north sides, but tall shrubs and trees planted inside fencing shielded it from view. The school itself blocked anyone on the south side from seeing the parking areas. The only road that offered a view of them was a narrow access road between the school and the football field.

"Plenty of people know it's there," Nadine said.

"So I take it you don't think there's a connection between the coach's death and the changes in Josh."

"Well, he got more withdrawn after that," Nadine said. "But it started before then. It just took Wayne a long time to believe me. And only a suspicious man like him would think it relates to the coach's death. As if our son had something to do with it."

Beckwell had never struck me as particularly suspicious, at least not more so than I imagined any homicide detective might be. But I'd never been married to him.

"What do you think caused the changes in Josh?"

A few robins hopped across the parkway between the café seating area and the street and cocked their heads at me. I shook the crumbs off my sandwich wrapper and they darted toward them.

"Wayne doesn't want to hear it, but Josh doesn't want to play basketball anymore. He won't say so. Not after he got that scholarship. But it's obvious to me."

"What makes you think he doesn't want to play?"

More robins joined the feeding frenzy. I liked watching these birds, so much smaller and more colorful than the plump gray pigeons that flocked to Chicago's outdoor plazas.

"He's not happy," Nadine said. "Hasn't been for most of the year. If you're not happy when you're winning that says it all, doesn't it?"

"Nothing changed other than the team winning?"

"His friend Anthony quit the team. His best friend. I think Josh is jealous that Anthony's dad let him quit and Josh has to keep playing."

I shifted my phone to the other hand. "Wayne won't let him leave the team?"

"Oh, he wouldn't stop him. But he'd be so disappointed. Feel Josh was wasting his talents. So would my husband, to tell the truth."

I went through something similar with acting. It was the one thing about me, along with singing, that drew my mother, at least temporarily, out of the dark fog of depression and anxiety she lived in. It made it hard for me to choose a different path, as I guessed, correctly, that nothing I did after that would excite her. Or, as it turned out, so much as interest her.

"Have you talked to Josh about it?"

"Ever tried to talk to a teenager? They won't say a word to an adult. I've tried, believe me."

From experience I knew that wasn't true. My niece and nephew told me plenty of things they didn't tell their parents.

We talked a while longer, but Nadine had nothing to add to what Wayne had already told me about the coach's death. Before I ended the call, though, she told me I might learn something at the football field. Once she explained why, I agreed.

I wished for different clothes. Ones that blended with those of the people around me.

Most parents sitting in the bleachers wore mid-thigh beige or tan cuffed shorts. The women paired them with pastel-colored fitted T-shirts and the men with yellow, red, or green short-sleeved polo shirts, some with pockets at the chest. I, on the other hand, carried my light-weight gray blazer, perfect for the airconditioned auditorium, and wore skinny jeans and a plain white tank top. Even my shoes marked me as an out-of-place city person: black ballet flats rather than athletic shoes.

Nadine told me these parents followed all the St. Angelina news, especially about the athletic departments, as they planned for their kids to attend in a year or two. These kids, now in junior high, were playing a practice game as part of a summer sports camp.

Though I kept my eyes on the field, I listened to the conversations around me. Nothing related to the basketball team, so I meandered to another part of the bleachers. After doing that twice, I finally caught part of a conversation about basketball.

I sat behind them and, after a moment, leaned forward. "Excuse me. I heard you mention the new basketball coach. Is he as good as Coach Taylor was?"

The man had pudgy fingers and a shade more razor stubble than could be considered fashionable. He twisted to look at me. "Matusek? As good as Taylor? Doubt it. He was assistant coach for years, and they passed him over to bring Taylor in. But they're stuck with him now while they look for someone else."

"Why pass him over?" I said, wondering how much resentment that had bred. But surely the police considered whether the assistant coach might have attacked Coach Taylor.

"Zack Taylor was a real basketball coach." The woman was thinner than the man and, at least sitting, taller, with a sharp nose and chin. She wore a pink T-shirt, but it was brighter than those of the other women nearby. "Not one of these multi-sport coaches. He has to – had to – coach everything. But basketball was his sport."

Pudgy fingers nodded. "He made a real commitment to the players. Expected one in return."

"What's that mean, a real commitment?"

Pink T-shirt eyed me, then gestured toward the field. "You have kids?"

"No, I'm volunteering with the summer theater program. But my, uh, nephew plays basketball. I thought I'd learn more about the school athletic department while I'm here."

I'd hesitated because it's easier to stick with a cover story based in truth, yet my nephew's athletic interests are limited to soccer, and my niece's to skateboarding. So I'd been thinking of, Eric, the teenage son of my former boyfriend, the one whose death I'd helped investigate. Eric plays high school basketball and loves it. But I didn't know how to quickly explain that relationship.

Not that these people cared. But it's one of many ways grief upends day-to-day life. I've never gotten used it, though I ought to be. For as long as I can remember, I've struggled with how to answer questions about whether I have siblings. Do I say I have one sister? Two but one died before I was born? Most people don't need to know that, but it feels wrong no matter how I answer.

"The coach used commitment contracts. You

heard of them?" Pudgy Fingers said.

I shook my head.

"Paper they sign promising to be at every practice on time, sleep enough hours, work out, eat right."

The woman's head bobbed. "That's right. No more slackers. If they weren't improving, or didn't put in the hours, they were out."

"Did any kids quit because of it?" I thought of Josh's friend. Maybe it had been too much for him. And was too much for Josh.

The man spread his hands wide. "Who would quit? The team finally won games, had a real shot at the championship."

"All because of this coach?"

The articles I read gave Coach Taylor credit for the turnaround, but I wanted the parents' take on it.

"He focused on the best players. And they came through when the bumblers were weeded out," the woman said. "No more of that everybody plays crap."

"But wouldn't you want to know your child would get a chance to play?"

The woman frowned. "If your kid's bad, sure. But ours is good. Our oldest. We liked him being on a winning team for a change."

"The previous coach, Coach Taylor. I heard he was killed in the faculty parking lot," I said.

"Mugging," the woman said. "Terrible. Right during the pep rally."

"Why wasn't he at the rally?" I said. It was something I'd forgotten to ask Nadine.

"He was there for a while," the man said. "But he and Matusek, I think they had a good cop bad cop thing going. Taylor was the tough guy, pushed the players to win. Matusek bought them dinners, gave them pep talks. Celebrated with them."

It sounded like some pretty high level manipulation to me.

"It must have been terrible for the girls who found him," I said. "I heard it was two cheerleaders."

I hadn't heard it, I'd read it, but close enough. The girls found the coach face down on the blacktop. His wallet lay nearby, open, no cash or credit cards inside. Knuckle abrasions and bruises on his jaw and cheekbone suggested a fight. Given his size – six foot five and over two hundred pounds – and athletic ability, I guessed more than one mugger. Though being big isn't a guarantee a criminal can't get the best of you.

The woman nodded. "It was awful. I bet

Kayla regrets getting them that pass."

"Kayla?" I said.

"McNulty. The cheerleading mentor. She was devastated. For more reasons than one, I'm guessing."

"Hannah, really?" the man said.

"What do you mean?" I said.

She leaned around her husband and lowered her voice. "I shouldn't say, but I saw her in Coach Taylor's office more than once. Very intense conversations. My friend was with me, and she's sure they were involved and it went bad."

The man frowned. "Why gossip about the poor woman? All you girls snipe, snipe, snipe, just because there's a pretty counselor."

She shrugged. "I'm telling you. You could have cut the tension with a knife. Maybe it wasn't a mugging at all. Maybe she had a jealous boyfriend who jumped him in the parking lot."

It wasn't impossible. But while I'd never gone to or worked in a high school, I didn't doubt gossip worked the same way, which meant grains of truth grew and distorted with every retelling.

A whistle blew, indicating half time. After making a mental note to find Kayla McNulty on the school website, I slipped away. Time to find Josh.

4

A KID WEARING gray sweats with the basketball team logo on them stopped me at south door to the gym. He studied my volunteer badge, then glanced down at my ballet flats and asked what I was doing there.

"Just checking out the space," I said. "My first day."

"Stay on the community side," he said. "These drills, sometimes balls go flying pretty hard. You don't want to get hit. And stick to the edges. You can't wear those shoes on the court."

"I'll be careful," I said.

In the gym the smell of pine layered over that of rubber mats and sweat. The basketball court was split in two. Four nets had been folded down, two each on the long sides of the gym. A few adults, I assumed parishioners, played a half-hearted game of Horse. A few kids shot baskets opposite them.

On the other half of the gym, kids dribbled as they wove around stacks of sand bags.

From where I stood, it was hard to pick out Josh Beckwell. Social media photos showed a tall, dark-haired boy with long limbs, very white teeth, and an easy smile. I edged around the open half of the court and sat on the bleachers as near as I could to the players. A few of the boys had dark hair, but the only one whose face resembled Josh's looked not much taller than I am, and I'm five seven. Josh stood six feet, two inches, according to Wayne.

A tall, angular man with reddish-blond hair stood on the sidelines. He wore blue gym shorts and a white St. Angelina's T-shirt. A whistle hung around his neck, and he held a clipboard he consulted every few minutes. Though I hadn't memorized all the faculty photos, Edward Matusek was the only red-haired male faculty member.

Matusek strode over to me a few minutes after I settled onto the bleachers. "Can I help you?"

His nametag confirmed he was Edward Matusek, which was good since he didn't introduce himself.

"Just watching," I said.

"I see that. Why are you watching my team?"

"Isn't this open gym?" I stood and held out my hand. "Quille Davis, a new volunteer. Just trying to get to know the school better."

He squeezed my fingers and released them in an instant. "Volunteer where?"

"Theater department. But one of my friend's sons is on your team. Josh Beckwell? I was hoping to say hello."

The corners of his mouth turned down, creating faint lines around his lips. "So was I."

"You were expecting him?" I said. "Are team members required to be here?"

If so, it fit with Beckwell's concern that Josh was losing interest.

Matusek glared at me. "Of course not. This is a dead period."

"What's a dead period?"

"You don't know?"

"I know next to nothing about basketball."

Not quite true, as I had seen a number of Eric's games. But I didn't know what a dead period was.

Coach Matusek's grip on the clipboard loosened enough that the color came back into his knuckles. "Athletes need breaks. Especially high school athletes. Helps avoid injuries. Allows them to be more well-rounded. If they want to play in off-season, they can, but it's never required."

His attention shifted to the court where a player, red-haired like the coach, stumbled into a pile of sandbags. I wondered if he might be the coach's son. The basketball rolled behind him, nearly tripping the next boy in line, who dodged at the last second.

The coach blew his whistle so close to my ear I jerked away in pain.

"Break," the coach yelled. "You, Drooler, take an extra time through alone. Work on coordination."

Drooler. This was the boy Rima, the girl in the theater class, mentioned. The one who started the oinking. He must love basketball to keep coming to open gym despite the team, and apparently the new coach, making fun of him.

The kid got to his feet and chased after his ball. Other than a red spot on his knee where he'd gone down, he didn't look hurt. Matusek blew the whistle again and the boy began weaving his way through the sandbags as the others watched.

"You think Josh will be here tomorrow?" I asked the coach. "So I can say hi?"

"He bet – probably will. He loves open gym. All the team members do."

I felt sure the coach was about to say "He better be." These dead periods must be serious, and the coach didn't want to give the impression he was making the kids play.

I tried to think of a way to ask about whether the guidance counselor, Kayla McNulty, ever argued with Coach Taylor. But I couldn't imagine any natural segue to that question.

Matusek glanced at the players and blew his whistle again. "All right, clear the court and we'll play." He turned to me. "If you're staying sit on the other side. You don't want to get hit by overthrown balls."

Everyone was so concerned about me.

"I will," I said.

Streetlights and floodlights from the school bathed the nearly-deserted student parking lot, leaving few shadows. The gated faculty lot where

I had parked was similarly bright. I wondered if it had been that way the night Coach Taylor was killed or if, like the fencing and cameras, more lights had been added.

It was after nine by the time I merged onto the Stevenson Expressway. Thankfully, traffic was light, never a given anymore heading into or out of downtown Chicago. My friend Lauren's car, a Volvo her parents bought her, handled beautifully. I appreciated that, as I don't drive all that often, and it helps to have a car that's easy to maneuver.

Less than half an hour after leaving the school I parked on the ground floor of the loft condo building where I live. Lauren lives in the same building. No parking spots were available for sale when she bought her unit, but it works out. I own a spot and Lauren owns a car, so we share both.

After texting for a while with my boyfriend about my day, I found Kayla McNulty on the school's website. She was a guidance counselor and had earned her Masters' degree a year ago. Other than an internship at another Catholic high school, St. Angelina's appeared to be her first employer. A quick check of the other two counselors showed they, too, doubled in some way in the athletics department. One was a tennis coach. The other ran the school's intramural program for kids who didn't make the school teams but still liked to play.

When I called Beckwell, he sounded surprised Josh hadn't gone to open gym.

"Coach Matusek didn't seem too happy about it." I curled in the corner of my couch, the phone on speaker on the steamer trunk next to me, my iPad propped on my knees.

"If he's anything like Coach Taylor, he wasn't. He wanted team members there four nights a week."

"Matusek said it's not required. That this is a rest period."

"Not required," Beckwell said. "But expected. If you see what I mean."

"I do." The law firm where I first practiced boasted that it had no billable hour requirement. But everyone knew if you didn't put in at least forty hours a week that could be billed to clients, which generally meant you worked around fifty or fifty-five hours total, you'd soon be looking for a new job.

I asked what Beckwell knew about Matusek, which turned out to be very little, other than seeing him at a few of the games. He couldn't recall Josh mentioning the former assistant coach. "But Josh liked the head coach before Taylor. Thought he was a nice guy. Though Josh was disappointed the team didn't do better."

I typed notes as Beckwell talked. "And Coach Taylor?"

"Josh never said much about him, either."

Beckwell did know Kayla McNulty, who was Josh's guidance counselor this year.

"Have you asked her if she's noticed a change in Josh?" I shifted position on the couch, nearly knocking the iPad to the floor.

"My ex did. Kayla encouraged Josh to come and see her, and I think he did a few times."

"Kayla – that's what you call her?"

He had used last names for both coaches.

"It's how she introduced herself. She said she wants students to see her as a friend. Doesn't like titles."

"There's not a particular title for guidance counselors, is there?"

"I guess she didn't like being Miss or Ms. McNulty."

I wondered if it felt too old to her. Her bio suggested she was only twenty-four or twenty-five. I'm used to being called "Ms. Davis" or "counsel" in court, but otherwise I still tend to tell people to use my first name. And "Miss Davis" reminds me of a sarcastic director who used to call me that when he was angry.

"Any problem with my talking to Kayla?" I said.

"She won't be able to tell you about Josh. It's confidential. She can talk to us about him, but not strangers."

"That's fine," I said. "I'm hoping to learn more about the school and the crime."

I decided against asking him if he'd heard rumors about Kayla and Coach Taylor. If he had, I felt sure he would have mentioned it. And if not, I didn't want my question getting back somehow to Kayla. It wouldn't make her inclined to open up to me. I also opted not to share Beckwell's ex-wife Nadine's view that Josh wanted to quit the team. They likely had had that conversation before. Many times. And if not, I didn't want him calling her and telling her I'd passed on what she said.

I did ask him about Josh's friend who quit the team.

"Anthony? He didn't quit. Coach Taylor cut him. Best thing for him if you ask me. He was the star player at his grade school, but it was a tiny school that could barely put together a team."

I highlighted Anthony's name. "Might someone say that about Josh being at this small high school?"

"He got a scholarship to a Division I school, Quille."

"Is Division I a big deal?"

I vaguely recalled Eric mentioning divisions when talking about a teammate who hoped to play college ball. Eric liked playing, but he didn't plan on continuing after high school except for fun.

Beckwell heaved a sigh at my relative ignorance of the sports world. "Yes, a big deal. So is the scholarship. Only two percent of high school basketball players get them. So when I say Josh is a star, it's not just because I'm his dad."

My low back started aching. I moved from my couch to a stool at my kitchen island. "And Anthony – not a star?"

"Average. Even Coach Guzman, the one before Taylor, didn't play him all that much. Josh told me the poor kid was convinced he could get a scholarship, too, if only Taylor played him more."

"Josh called him a poor kid?" I typed the words after Anthony's name with a question mark.

"No, that's me. Josh just told me about Anthony thinking he could get a scholarship."

"Did Josh think Anthony was good?"

"Nah. He'd never say it, he's too nice a kid. But he knew his friend was only so-so."

"Did Josh ever pick on Anthony? Or other kids?"

"Josh? Not that I heard."

"So the changes in him you and your ex have been seeing – no disciplinary issues?"

"None."

If Rima was right, though, there wouldn't be any. At most, Josh might have run extra sprints during practice.

I scrolled through my notes. "Why do you think it's good that Anthony got cut?"

"End the delusions of grandeur. Let him spend his time on something he might be good at."

"What if he just liked playing? For the fun of it."

"He can play with his friends. Believe me, it's no fun to sit on the bench."

"Speaking from experience?"

"One year of college football. During which I played a total of eighteen minutes."

I filled a glass from the faucet and took a long

drink as I thought about what else Beckwell could help with.

"Do you have a photo of Anthony? If he loves playing, maybe he goes to the open gym. He might talk to me about Coach Taylor."

Anyone with a grudge at the very least might have something to say.

"Must have one somewhere," Beckwell said. "Or Nadine will. I'll text you."

My phone buzzed as I finished washing my face and changing into one of the long T-shirts I sleep in during the summer. Beckwell had sent three photos, but I only needed one.

Anthony was the stumbling red-haired boy the coach had called Drooler.

5

—————

DURING THE SCHOOL year it would have been easy to talk with Kayla McNulty. I could have dropped in at her office or at least lingered outside the guidance department. But the guidance offices department was dark when I arrived early the following day.

Instead I hunted down Polly, catching her as she locked her office door.

"My niece is thinking of going to college to become a guidance counselor," I said. "I was hoping I could talk with someone here about what it's like, but the Department's closed."

The claim about my niece was only a bit of a stretch. At seventeen, she was exploring multiple career options and texted me often with questions. While she hadn't mentioned being a high school guidance counselor, she was thinking of majoring in psychology.

Polly gripped her script, full of red markings. "They have the same contracts we do. So summers off unless, like me, you take on a part-time gig."

"If I emailed one of the counselors, would they get it? I was thinking Kayla McNulty since I saw she's a recent college graduate."

"They're not required to check school email during the summer."

"You don't happen to have another way to reach her, do you?" I said.

"No. Go on ahead, will you? Start the students on warmups if I'm not there on time. I need to make a stop."

"Sure."

A young man I recognized as Josh Beckwell barred the door to the auditorium. He looked both thinner and taller than I had expected based on his photos, surprising since often a camera makes a person look heavier. His dark brown hair swept back from a face with a square jaw, clear skin, and hazel eyes rimmed by thick lashes that must be the envy of every girl at the high school.

"Quille?" he said.

"Yes. Josh?" I put out my hand. "I'm a friend of your dad's."

His fingers grazed mine, then he crossed his arms over his chest. "You got me in trouble."

"Trouble? With who?"

"Coach Matusek doesn't like people spying on practice."

Clearly there was nothing "open" about open gym.

"I'm sorry. I wanted to see the gym and introduce myself to you."

"Why?"

I glanced at the time on my phone. "In fifteen minutes, I need to start a rehearsal. Can we talk when I'm done? I'd buy you a coffee or soda but the form I signed last week tells me it's against the rules."

While the principal hadn't asked me many questions, he had been very clear about the importance of avoiding inappropriate contact with students. Making me wonder if there were incidents I ought to know about.

Josh shrugged. "Rules don't apply to the basketball team."

"But they apply to me. How about before your open gym. Or after?"

"No. Don't come around there again."

The hallway was deserted, but I didn't want anyone else to overhear.

"I guess we'll talk now. Let's walk outside for a few minutes." I headed for a side door as if I took it for granted he would follow me. He did.

We stood on a narrow strip of lawn across the road from the football field.

"Did your dad tell you what he asked me to do?"

"Mom says you and dad think someone killed the coach."

"Someone did kill the coach."

Another shrug. "A mugger."

"You believe that?"

"Why wouldn't I?"

The sun felt hot, and I slipped my sweater off. "You don't know of anyone angry at Coach Taylor?"

"Players he cut from the team. Their parents. Doesn't mean someone killed him."

"What did you think of him?"

Josh watched a garbage truck rumble down

the access road between the school and the foot-ball field. "We had a great season. Won some games in the state tournament. Finally. How'd Dad rope you into this, anyway?"

"We crossed paths a few times involving crimes. Starting with my former boyfriend's death. I've helped your dad a couple times, and he's helped me."

"Your boyfriend died?"

Ty, my current boyfriend, was very much alive, but Josh didn't need details about my personal life.

"About a year and a half ago," I said. "That's when I met your dad."

"What, and you, like figured out the crime? When my dad didn't?" His eyes brightened, clearly intrigued by the idea that I might have bested his father. It made me think Nadine could be right that Josh kept playing because his dad insisted on it.

"In a way. I can tell you about it sometime. But right now, I need to know about Coach Taylor. Did you like him?"

His chin jutted forward. "No one likes a good coach. He makes you work."

"Like the stage manager."

"The what?"

"That's the person in theater who makes sure everything gets done before and during a play, including the actors being on time."

He angled his body toward me for the first time. "Do they tell you everything you did wrong?"

"Sometimes, yes. Though the director does that, too."

"So you're a real actor?"

"Was. I'm a lawyer now."

Now he faced me directly. "You quit?"

"That's how my mom puts it. I think of it as choosing a different profession. Why?"

He glanced away again, studying an oak tree with wide, spreading branches. "Just curious."

"Are you thinking you might want to play pro ball?"

"No."

"But you're planning on it for college?"

"Yeah."

This kid would do better than most of my clients in a deposition. That's where the opposing lawyer asks a witness questions under oath. The rule, if you're the witness, is to answer each question as briefly as possible and never volunteer anything that wasn't asked.

"When did you first meet Coach Taylor?"

"Tryouts last fall."

I glanced at my phone again. Rehearsal started in five minutes. "Did he run them differently than the previous coach?"

A faint twitch of the shoulders. "Told us every position was up for grabs. No one on last year's team was guaranteed a spot. Some people didn't believe him."

"Your dad told me one of your friends didn't make the team. Was that why?"

Josh huffed out a breath. "He did make it. But later he got cut. He didn't take the coach seriously."

"What should he have done that he didn't do?"

"Played better."

"So he came to practice, he did all the things everyone on the team agreed to do, but he just wasn't good enough?"

"Right. The old coach kept him on out of charity. That's what Coach Taylor said. If everyone gets to play, everyone gets to lose."

"So that saying about it's not if you win or lose, it's how you play the game – that doesn't apply to basketball?"

Josh's laugh sounded more like a bark. "Doesn't apply to life."

"Something else Coach Taylor said?"

"He's right. Anthony's dad thought he should get a scholarship too. He wasn't going to get that without winning."

"But you did. The team wasn't winning much, but you got a scholarship."

He glared at me. "Anthony wasn't good, okay? Nothing I could do. We practiced together all the time and he just wasn't that good."

"I'm sorry, I shouldn't have said it that way. It's not your fault Anthony wasn't a better player or that he couldn't stay on the team. Sometimes people love things and they can't do them professionally. I had an actor friend where that was an issue."

And he wasn't my friend anymore, but I didn't think that would help Josh to hear.

"Well, Anthony's not mad at me."

If true, I hoped Josh would introduce me to Anthony. I figured he might have a lot to say about Coach Taylor. But I decided to wait until the next time I talked to Josh to ask. Right now I wanted to get the big picture and, I hoped, leave him seeing me as a friendly face.

"What about the rest of the team? I heard they make fun of kids that were cut."

Josh shifted from one foot to the other and

crossed his arms over his chest. "Every team's got jerks."

"Also just like life," I said.

My smartphone trilled, telling me I had three minutes left to get inside. I told Josh I had to go, but that I'd be there every day for rehearsal. I urged him to stop by so we could talk more. "And your mom and dad have my number. I'll talk any time you want."

I wanted to give it to him myself, but the rules only allowed faculty to do that for students in their classes. In my case, that meant only the theater students.

"Thanks," he said.

I wasn't sure what he was thanking me for. But I hoped it meant he would come talk with me again.

———

Polly was about fifteen minutes late. I used the time to show the students some enunciation exercises I learned as an actor and still used sometimes before key court arguments. Something I shared with the students, less for them and more as ammunition against parents who might question them spending time on theater.

In class, we worked on blocking, where actors walk through stage directions and learn where to be and what to do at all times during the play. The student assistant director took over for a while and Polly turned to me. "The principal wants to see you when we're done."

"Why?"

"No idea. I saw him and he asked how things were going with you, then told me to tell you to come by at 4:45."

"That's before we're done," I said.

Polly waved toward the stage. "I think I can get by without you for fifteen minutes."

It struck me as particularly odd that Principal Scott Galleti wanted to see me after how little interest he showed during our first meeting. Maybe Polly hadn't so much run into him as gone to see him to ask about me.

6

"Miss Davis, have a seat," the principal said when I arrived at 4:45. His office, while a little larger than Polly's, looked much like hers, featuring the same large crucifix on the wall and the same wood and metal office furniture. He sat ramrod straight, his expression serious.

I threaded my way around stacks of files to his single visitor chair. "Call me Quille."

"Why were you at the gym last Monday night?"

Everyone wanted to know.

"Isn't everyone welcome at open gym?"

"Everyone's welcome to *use* the gym. Coach Matusek said you were watching the team practice."

Matusek made clear the sessions weren't team practice. They ought to get their messaging straight.

"I wanted to see more of the school. I never attended high school, so I'm always curious about it."

He frowned. "You're a lawyer but you never attended high school?"

"I did independent study. To make it easier to fit around my acting."

"You were home schooled."

"Something like that."

I rarely said I was home-schooled because a lot of people thought it meant my parents limited what I was allowed to study. But while my Gram helped me plan and my dad insisted on my taking standardized tests to be sure I kept up, I designed my own coursework and, when I reached college, discovered I'd read more widely and learned more than most of my classmates. My mom, who struggled with anxiety and depression, spent time with me on singing and running lines, but not schoolwork. It exhausted her.

"So you were just interested?" Galleti said.

"Yes. Don't parents ever come and watch their kids practice?" I said.

"Oh, they do. That's the trouble. The coach is under a lot of pressure."

"Pressure to perform as well as Coach Taylor? That must be stressful."

Galleti rubbed his forehead. "You've no idea. Half the parents are angry Taylor cut their kids from the team and are begging Matusek to give them another chance. Half are afraid Matusek won't be demanding enough and the team will go soft. And the other half send endless emails of advice, including to me." His hand dropped onto the desk. "And I realize that's too many halves. But that's how it seems. They call, they text, they email, they pound out comments in capital letters on social media."

"Did parents contact Coach Taylor, too?"

"A lot of the same ones. How dare he cut their kids. But the other half were encouraging. Thrilled about the team winning."

"So only two halves for Coach Taylor?"

The principal smiled at last. "When a team's winning, parents don't feel so much like they need to give advice."

"What about students? I heard when the team started winning some players became, let's say, not the nicest of people."

Galleti grimaced. "Teenagers can be mean,

Miss Davis. You may not quite understand how they are as a group since you didn't attend high school. But there are always In groups and Out groups. No one likes being out. The basketball players got made fun of for years for being losers. So did some behave badly when they got to be on top of the heap? Of course. But we dealt with it."

"How?"

"How what?"

"How did you deal with it? I'm curious. Not having attended high school."

His eyes narrowed as if he were uncertain whether I was being sarcastic. I waited, keeping my lips in a half-smile, my body posture relaxed but angled forward to suggest curiosity.

"Coach Taylor dealt with it. Extra sprints, calisthenics. And he told them they needed to behave like champions, be role models."

Not radically different from what the theater student, Rima, told me happened to team members.

"I'm sorry if I disturbed Coach Matusek."

"He'll get over it."

"I wonder if you could help me with something. My niece and nephew are almost high school age. I was hoping to learn more about what it's like being a guidance counselor. My

niece is interested, and I thought since I'm here.
..."

I deliberately trailed off to see if he might fill in the blanks and mention Kayla. At which point I'd know that Polly had told him about my questions.

But he was too smart for that, or she hadn't told him. "Anyone in particular you hoped to talk with?"

"Your website says Kayla McNulty's the newest. Maybe her? But anyone would be helpful."

"I'll send her your contact information. She can get in touch if she wants to."

"Great." I stood. "Thank you."

My hand was on the doorknob to leave when Galleti said, "Any reason you were asking about Josh Beckwell?"

I turned sideways to look at him. "I'm a friend of the family. Hoping to say hello."

"Right, right. That's how you came to us."

Somehow I doubted he'd forgotten that. "Yes."

"Nadine is a key board member. She spoke highly of you."

"Good to know. If you could pass my information on to Kayla McNulty I'd really appreciate it."

"Of course. Polly said you're doing a great job, by the way."

Now I knew Polly had spoken to him, but I left unsure whether she complained about my asking after Kayla, praised me, or both.

7

———————

My Gram still owns the apartment building in LaGrange where I grew up, and she lives in the same apartment. After agreeing to help Beckwell, I had called to ask her to see what she could learn. She followed local news and knew a lot of people in the near west suburbs.

When I let myself in, I found her at the stove. The kitchen smelled of ham or bacon. Her short white hair formed perfect waves around her face. The sleeves of her button-down olive green shirt were rolled up, and she wore pin-striped gray pants and low-heeled sandals. Though no customers see her at the lighting store where she works as a bookkeeper, she always dresses as if they might.

We caught up as she finished making dinner, and I set the table in the small dining alcove off the kitchen. Last year Gram had replaced its worn hardwood floor with black and white tile that simultaneously gave it a classic and updated feel.

Once we sat down to eat – ham plus macaroni and cheese and steamed asparagus – she told me someone in her bridge club had a son and a nephew at St. Angelina's. "The nephew's on the basketball team. All the parents were thrilled the team finally started winning."

"Did parents like Coach Taylor?"

"Not the ones whose kids ended up off the team. But from what she said, it sounded like the rest of them did. Grace said he knew how to motivate the kids. The previous coach was a namby-pamby who let them get away with anything."

I winced inwardly at the term, which I'd heard so often growing up. Gram had little patience for people who didn't get things done. Her drive inspired me. But it made her relationship with my parents a challenge in a way I hadn't recognized when I was a kid.

Gram understood my mother grieving over the death of my sister, but without saying so she conveyed that the failure to snap out of it had to do with lack of willpower. She also felt my dad ought to "cater" less to my mother. I don't think depression was something people talked about much when Gram was younger, and I doubted she understood much about it. Not that I had a perfect grasp of it. As an adult, I spent a lot of time struggling with my mother's lack of interest in me.

"Get away with anything? Like what?" I asked, thinking of Josh's comment that the rules didn't apply to the team.

"My impression? Losing. She meant losing."

I took another asparagus stalk and cut it into pieces. "I never think of losing as something you get away with."

"It is if you lose because you didn't work hard or try to improve. Coach Taylor made them sign something called commitment contracts."

"I heard about that. Did your friend say what happened if they didn't sign?"

"She didn't say. I suppose they were cut from the team."

"Did she know any kids who quit?"

Those were the students, along with ones like Josh's friend Anthony who'd been cut, who might be able to tell me the most about Coach Taylor.

"One of her son's friends. He took some art

class on Sunday mornings. The coach insisted he quit. That he couldn't have competing interests."

"That seems extreme for high school. Seems like kids ought to be exploring."

Gram pointed her fork in my direction. "You were pretty focused on acting at that age."

"Right. And it's not what I ended up doing. So it's good you pushed me to learn other things."

"I'd love to take credit, honey. But I thought you needed a broad education to be a good actress. And I wanted you to understand business so you could take of yourself and your finances."

"Whatever your reasons, it was a good thing. Did your friend say anything else?"

"No. I would have asked more, but she started wondering why I wanted to know." Gram went into the kitchen to refill her water glass. "It's not as if I'm a basketball fan. So I changed the subject."

"Good. I don't want anyone involved in the Coach's death to think you're asking too many questions."

Gram returned with a pitcher of water for the table. "I'll still keep my ears open."

"Just promise you won't say anything that could make anyone suspicious."

She squeezed my shoulder. "I could say the same to you."

───────

I half-expected the principal to ignore my request about Kayla McNulty. But she texted me the next day, and we arranged to meet that night. To my surprise, she lived in Greektown, a neighborhood a mile or so west of downtown Chicago. During the school year she probably took the train each day into Riverside.

Since I didn't need to be at the school late, I took the train myself that day. My return train arrived at Union Station at 5:55 in the evening. A five-minute walk and I was in Greektown. Historically home to Greek immigrants, the area still includes Greek restaurants and shops, but also a mix of loft condos and businesses.

Kayla had chosen Artopolis, a restaurant on Halsted Street. The wall facing the street folded back in good weather, giving the front seating area with its small round tables the feel of an indoor/outdoor sidewalk café. It had been a while since I'd been there, but I remembered loving the kourabiedes, Greek butter cookies made with almonds and coated with powdered sugar. I bought a box every year during Greek Fest, one of my favorite city summer festivals.

Kayla got there a few minutes after I did. She was about five inches shorter than me with very blond, very curly hair, a heart-shaped face, and a trim build. Her wrap dress featured a drawing of tulips. "So your niece is considering becoming a counselor?"

"Among many other things," I said. "But I'm hoping she might move here, or at least nearer to me, when she finishes school, so I really appreciate the perspective of someone working in the area."

That part at least was true. Other than Gram, I was closest to my niece and nephew in my family, and I would love if either or both of them decided to live in Chicago during or after college.

The waiter brought over menus. Kayla knew Greek wines better than I did, and we discovered we both liked slightly jammy Pinot Noirs. I suggested she choose a bottle. Two drinks is pretty much my limit, and usually I wouldn't drink that much with a stranger. But conversation flows more freely over a bottle of wine.

"Well, I'm happy to share what I can," she said after the waiter disappeared. "I've only been a counselor for a year. And the market's tough these days, part of why I'm at St. Angelina's. Nothing against Catholic schools. I grew up Catholic. But the suburban public school pay is much better."

"Are you thinking you'll switch at some point?"

"Well, right now I share a one-bedroom with two other girls. It's the only way I can afford to live in the city, which I love. So probably, yes, if I can."

That might explain how easily she took me up on my offer to buy her dinner if she was willing to meet and tell me about guidance counseling as a career.

"How are the students?" I said.

"Oh, I like them a lot."

"They seem great," I said. "That's kind of why I started volunteering. I'm friends with one of their dads. Josh Beckwell's."

"Oh, that's you? Josh mentioned a friend of his parents was volunteering." She leaned closer. "He's a little worried you're there to spy on him."

"No spying, I promise."

The waiter returned with our wine and took our orders, giving me a few moments to think. This was the second time someone talked about spying. Also, Beckwell approached me after the end of the school year. Kayla wasn't working for the summer. Which meant she talked to Josh outside the normal school relationship.

The wine tasted a little too tart for me, but it was still good. "Josh's dad is a little concerned about safety," I said. "With the coach's death happening at school."

I figured that way of framing it fit whatever Josh had told her without revealing that Beckwell hoped I'd sort out what had happened.

"Everyone is. That parking lot, I hated it at night."

"Didn't some students find him there?"

She shuddered. "Two of my cheerleaders. The student lot's farther from the school, and before the coach's death both parking areas were really dark at night. So I got the girls passes to the faculty lot as often as I could if there were night games or practices. Really regretted that."

"I'm so sorry."

We talked about that for a while, but nothing she told me differed from the news articles I'd read.

The waiter brought out our Taramasalata appetizer, a fish roe dip with olives and bread. As we ate, I asked more questions about being a guidance counselor, sipping my first glass of wine slowly so as to stay clearheaded. Kayla finished her second glass by the time the main courses arrived.

"Seems like Coach Taylor was very popular," I said, wanting to gauge her reaction.

She cut into her lemon chicken. "Who told you that?"

"Wayne Beckwell. He said how happy the parents were to have a winning team at last."

"Winning, yes. Popular, no. He was terrible to those kids."

"Terrible? How?"

"Berating them if they lost. Sometimes when they won. Calling them names. And kids who left the team, they became like non-people."

"The coach didn't talk to them anymore?"

"Barely. If they were in his gym class, he'd motion to them what to do. But if he had to give directions verbally, he told one of his team members to tell those kids. And I'm not betraying any student confidences here. I heard him myself when I passed by the gym. No one ever accused that man of being quiet."

"Did you talk to him about it?"

"Right then." She waved her fork. "Looking back, bad idea. He was so mad I did it in front of his class. Said it undermined him. Galleti came down on me for it, too. Told me to stay out of the athletics department. Which shows what he thinks of cheerleading."

"It's part of the athletics department?"

"That's what the school website says, but what do I know?"

If there was more than one confrontation with Coach Taylor, it might explain the heated conversations the woman at the football field overheard.

"Had you tried talking to Coach Taylor before?'

"Oh, yes. Did no good. He said who cares what a girl with a psych degree barely out of college thinks?"

"Nice."

"Oh, yes. I needed a Master's to get a job as a guidance counselor, by the way, not that he cared."

"And Scott Galleti? As the principal, he ought to be concerned about the students," I said.

"Tried a couple times with him. But he just called the coach's approach old-style, said he'd talk to him about toning it down. I'm pretty sure he thought the parents preferred Taylor over the last coach. He didn't seem to care that I'm hearing directly from students, and they tell me things they won't tell their parents."

"Are guidance counselors allowed to pass on what students say?"

As a lawyer, I can't share anything a client tells me other than in extremely limited circumstances, such as to prevent a murder. My online research showed the rules were similar for therapists, but the lines were fuzzier for high school counselors.

"I can share if it's to prevent harm to others or self-harm. If we're talking physical harm, it's easy to know what I can say. When it comes to psychological harm, that's a tougher call. Especially if you think it may get back to a bully, yet nothing will be done about it, and he'll take it out on the student."

"And you think Coach Taylor was a bully?"

"No question. But he was a bully who got results, and for a lot of people that's what matters. Galleti told me the only parents who complained were the ones whose kids got cut from the team."

"But you heard things from players who were on the team?"

She fiddled with the stem of her wineglass. "I really can't say who told me or what they said. But I had concerns."

I finished the last swallow of my wine. "That has to be a tough part of the job."

She nodded, and I asked more about what schools looked for in counselors, hoping she didn't find my interest in Coach Taylor odd.

As we ate dessert and polished off the last of wine in the bottle, I brought the conversation back to basketball.

"Josh said something to me about the rules not applying to basketball players. I've been wondering what he meant."

A gnat landed on the rim of Kayla's wine glass, a hazard of outdoor eating. Kayla swatted it away. "Oh, they get all sorts of perks. Coach Taylor started that. Pizza parties twice a month. Extra sprints or drills instead of detention. Passes to the faculty parking area – though that stopped after the coach's death. School clamped down on that."

The second mention of passes reminded me of what Nadine, Beckwell's ex-wife, had said about the changes to the parking lots.

"Passes, why did that matter? Someone told me the lots weren't gated back then."

"No, but students got detention if they parked there without a pass. And if they kept doing it, the car got towed. Which did not make the parents happy."

That meant more people with easy access to the faculty lot. But also records of cars that didn't belong there. I wondered if the police had looked at that.

I bit into one of my cookies. Powdered sugar scattered everywhere. As I wiped the table I thought about whether I wanted to ask one last question.

"I had to sign this form that I'd follow all the rules dealing with students," I said. "No contact that wasn't about class. No meetings with the door closed. And no giving out my home number." Which was, now that I thought of it, a little outdated. My Gram was one of the only people I knew who had a home phone anymore, and she rarely used it. "Do those rules apply to the team?"

Kayla tore the edges of her paper drink napkin. "Well, that all still applied to the team. That's a very strict school policy. Keeps there from being any inappropriate contact. But other rules, like don't bring coffee or soda into class, or no short sleeves, those don't apply."

"I've seen plenty of T-shirts," I said. I didn't care what students wore, but I wanted her to think my curiosity revolved around rules, not her or Josh.

"It's relaxed for the summer. T-shirts are okay so long as no slogans. Other than the school teams, of course."

"Of course."

I asked a few more general things about her work and picked up the check. Overall, I hoped I hadn't made her suspicious.

But it turned out I had.

8

"I HATE YOU." Josh spoke the second I emerged from rehearsal the next afternoon. I walked out after the students left, but with Polly right behind me.

"What's wrong? What happened?" I touched his elbow and motioned him to one side of the hall near the trophy cases as if I were trying to get us out of Polly's way.

"You grilled Kayla."

Another person calling the guidance counselor by her first name. And she must have texted or called him about meeting with me. Otherwise, there was no way he could know about it. I hadn't told Wayne or his ex-wife.

It added to an idea that had taken shape

during the dinner with Kayla, that there might be more to their relationship than counselor and student. I guessed Kayla, based on her appearance and bio, about five years older than Josh, who was a month short of his eighteenth birthday. Under Illinois law, if Kayla didn't have a faculty-like relationship with Josh, there was nothing criminal even if she had sex with him. But as a faculty member, it was different, which she likely knew.

The uneven power dynamic in that type of relationship also could explain Josh's mood changes and anger.

I waited until Polly disappeared around the corner to answer. "I'm trying to find out what anyone knows about the coach's death, that's all. I told you that."

"But you asked her about me."

"We talked about you. I don't remember who mentioned you first. Does it matter?"

"I don't want you to get her in trouble. She's the only one on my side."

"Why do you think I might get her in trouble?"

I also wanted to know what being on his side meant, but first things first.

"You're the one who told me about all these

rules. You tell me." He thrust his head forward toward me, his hands in fists at his sides. "Is there some rule that I can't be friends with Kayla?"

"Are you friends?"

"Answer me first."

"I don't know of any rule that says you can't be friends. But there are rules about faculty or staff or volunteers texting or calling students who aren't in their classes at the time."

"She's a guidance counselor. She doesn't have a class."

"No, but she isn't working this summer, is she?" His face reddened, so I added, "Still, I don't know how that rule applies with the guidance counselors. Maybe it doesn't."

"The coaches text us all the time. All the time. Why can't she?"

"Maybe they shouldn't do that," I said.

"Tell them that."

"Are you talking about Coach Taylor?"

"Him. Matusek. They're all the same."

"But the coach before Taylor, he wasn't like that?"

His lower lip stuck out, and despite his height for a second he looked like a lost child "I don't know. I don't remember. All I know is you better not get Kayla in trouble."

"You said she's the only one on your side. What do you mean?"

"She listens to me."

"Do you parents not listen?"

"No one does."

I was listening, but I doubted pointing that out would help. "Is this about the way the coaches treat players? Is that the way Kayla's on your side?"

"Just leave her alone." He stomped down the hall. I didn't follow. I couldn't think of anything else I could say right now that would make anything better.

I glanced at the time on my phone. Even at a fast walk, I'd miss the early train. I was texting Ty to let him know to come to my place later when Polly came around the corner.

"Why didn't you tell me you were here about the coach's death? Let's talk."

9

WE SAT in Polly's office with the door shut. She rolled her pen forward and back on her desk. "I knew you were here for something else. You're overqualified."

On first meeting, she had said my experience was outdated. The change made me wonder. "So why did you think I was here?"

"All that accounting in your background. I figured it was some sort of audit."

"Audit? It's not like the IRS sends people in undercover."

The pen rolled onto the floor. Polly retrieved it, straightened, and slid her chair back from her desk an inch or so. "Maybe the school's thinking of getting rid of the theater program altogether.

Cut the expense."

"No one asked me to look at expenses." I didn't buy her being worried about that. If the school wanted to look at expenses they only had to go through the books. They didn't need someone like me to come in and pretend to volunteer. But I was more interested for the moment in the coach's death. "So can you tell me anything about Coach Taylor?"

"He's a bully. Was. And Matusek is following suit from what I hear. He thinks it's the only way to win. Coaching through fear."

"And the team did win."

"But the players are miserable. Except the ones who are bullies themselves and enjoy getting free reign over the school."

"Team members talked to you about this?"

"One basketball player did. He tried out for the fall play. And made it. It was off season, but Coach Taylor told him absolutely not. No splitting his attention."

"I'm obviously fond of theater, too. But that doesn't make him a bully."

"It does if you call the kid a lot of names I won't say and imply he's a closeted gay and you'll out him for it."

"Is that something the students would ostracize him for?"

"A year ago, I would've said no. Despite the official Church position on a lot of issues, Saint Angelina's is pretty liberal. All about equal rights and social justice, and most of the students like that."

That fit with what my friend Lauren had told me about the Catholic Church in Chicago. She also said a lot of Catholics she knew disagreed with the Church on many things but still wanted to be part of it.

"Hard to believe one coach could change the entire culture of school," I said.

"Not the whole school. the team. And because sports matter, they can change the school. The meanest boys on the team would have made that kid's life a living hell."

"Is Josh one of the them?"

Polly shook her head. "Not that I know of. But he doesn't stop it."

"Could he?"

The dynamics of high school were a puzzle to me, but I guessed it couldn't be that different from any group of adults, minus some maturity and plus a lot of surging hormones. Which made me think it might be a lot like a mob. Once it moved in a certain direction, one person trying to stand against it got trampled.

"From what this boy told me, anyone who tried to stand up for the weaker kids risked getting kicked off the team. By Taylor anyway. Remains to be seen how far Matusek will go down that road."

If his mother was right and Josh did want to quit playing, he could stand up for a weaker kid because he wouldn't care about getting kicked off. In fact, it might solve his entire problem. But maybe he felt that would be a deeper disappointment to his dad and stepdad.

"I don't understand why the school lets this go on," I said.

"A winning team brings in more students, and Catholic schools are struggling to stay afloat."

"Did you tell the principal? About this student?"

"He spoke to me in confidence and begged me not to say anything. So I didn't give specifics about him. But I did tell Galleti my concerns. And that I thought Coach Taylor intimidated a lot of students. Most of them probably never said anything to anyone, including their parents."

I thought of Matusek's paranoia about me

watching, and Josh saying I got him in trouble with the coach. If Matusek followed Taylor's playbook, then Taylor, too, had made clear he didn't like players who involved their parents.

"But if no one says anything it just goes on."

She took off her glasses and rubbed her eyes. "I know. But suppose I did go against this student's wishes. It wouldn't prove anything. It's an old rivalry between sports and theater. Goes back decades. Made worse by funding cuts that always hit the arts harder."

"And what about Taylor's death? Do you know something?"

"The night before he died, I overheard him arguing with another man in the gym. Don't know for sure who. But they were talking, or shouting, about how Taylor treated one of the players."

"Do you know which one?"

"They said 'that kid,' so no."

"Who was the other man?"

"I don't know. His back was to me, and I only saw through a partly open door. They were in the far corner of the gym."

"If you had to guess?"

She glanced around as if someone else might have snuck into the office with us. "Coach Matusek. Because the man looked a few inches shorter than Taylor, heavier build, and his hair looked reddish. Plus Taylor kept saying he was the one who knew basketball, he'd decide what was right for the team. But with a lot of swearing interspersed."

"Unusual for Taylor?"

"At school. Faculty are supposed to be cautious about language. Though I've no idea what language he uses when it's just him and his team."

"Why does the knowing basketball part make you think the other man was Matusek?"

"His main sport was football, not basketball."

She told me she didn't hear anything else, and she did relay all of it to the police.

Polly rolled her pen again. "But Matusek never got arrested, so I guess it didn't pan out. Or they didn't take me seriously."

I doubted that. The Riverside police department might be small, but I couldn't imagine, however inexperienced with murder investigations, that they didn't question the assistant coach. He benefitted from Coach Taylor's death.

"What's your impression of Kayla McNulty?" I said.

"You think she killed the coach? She's so trim and tiny."

"I meant her relationship with the students."

"Like Josh? I heard what he said about her. But I don't think you need to worry. My theater kids love her, the ones lucky enough to be assigned to her. She really listens to them and relates."

"Do they all call her Kayla?"

"Every last one. Way too informal if you ask me, but that's probably my age talking." She brushed her silver-gray hair away from her face. "Things are different now."

I sat on a wrought iron bench in the shadow of the Riverside train station. The early evening sun still shone fairly hot, and the humid air smelled faintly of creosote from the railroad ties.

During rush hour, many trains run on the Burlington Northern Santa Fe line into downtown Chicago. After six, though, they only run once an hour, so I had time to kill.

After reviewing some documents for my law practice, I typed notes on my conversation with Polly into my iPad, then studied the cylindrical water tower on the other side of the tracks and let my thoughts drift. After a few minutes, it crossed my mind that Polly might have invented overhearing an argument to distract me from whatever it was that made her lock her office door.

But if Matusek had argued with Taylor, it still didn't help much. Because Polly also confirmed that Matusek was at the pep rally and took the team out that night for pizza. While he might have slipped away to the parking lot and returned, as with any students who attended the rally, it seemed likely he would have had noticeable injuries or blood on his clothes.

Bells clanged and a headlight appeared down the tracks to the west. I stood and walked toward where I thought the head train car was likely to stop. Once I got on, I needed to review a fifteen-page motion the other side had filed in one of my cases. My answer to it was due in four days, meaning other than rehearsal I couldn't spend much time poking around St. Angelina's during the rest of the week.

But there was one person I meant to talk to if I could. Josh's friend Anthony.

10

In a perfect world, Josh would have wanted to help me get in touch with Anthony, but I doubted he felt inclined to help me at the moment. Social media didn't reveal a lot. Anthony's Facebook posts were minimal. I texted my niece to ask her to look through other social networks, ones I might not be aware of. I used a couple platforms to talk about my law firm, but otherwise avoided being online. I'd had enough publicity as a child actress.

Two hours later my niece texted back that she couldn't find very much other than lots of photos with Anthony and his dad playing basketball. But she had learned Anthony worked early afternoons at an ice cream store in Oak Park, a suburb a few miles north of St. Angelina's.

By working two late nights and part of the weekend, I was able to take off early the following Monday. I drove to the ice cream shop. Anthony worked behind the counter. Light freckles covered his face and his arms. Like Josh, he was long-limbed. But I guessed him 5'10" at best and wondered if that was enough for college basketball.

There was a long line, so I ordered a chocolate malt and stationed myself at a table near the counter, hoping for a quiet time. While I waited, I ran invoices on my laptop.

Finally, when my malt was nearly gone, the store was empty of other customers. I approached the counter. Anthony was changing out an empty bin of strawberry cheesecake ice cream with a full one.

"Anthony?" I said.

"Huh?"

I introduced myself and told him I was a friend of Josh Beckwell's family and I'd like to talk to him.

"About what?"

"Your opinion about Coach Taylor." I was

hoping he had strong enough feelings that he'd be eager to talk. And wouldn't pause to wonder why I wanted to know.

After asking someone in the back if he could take a break, he slid into the chair across from me. "What d'you care about the coach?"

"Josh's dad is worried about him. He says Josh has changed a lot in the last year. And I think it might be because of Coach Taylor."

Beckwell had felt sure the two boys never spoke anymore. I was banking on that, otherwise my comments would get back to Josh and he'd see them as proof that I lied about being at the school to investigate the coach's death. That I could be there to do more than one thing probably wouldn't make him feel any better.

"That and he's a jerk," Anthony said.

"Josh is?"

"He is now."

"But he wasn't always?"

Anthony looked to one side, studying a photo of the ice cream shop crew that he must have seen hundreds of times before. "He was my best friend. Until I wasn't on the team anymore. Then he laughed at me."

"Josh did? Personally?"

Anthony's head dropped and he mumbled at the table. "All of them."

"But didn't I see you at practice the other night?"

"That's not practice. Or, you know, for the team it's practice. But it's also open gym. So everyone's saying joining in might be a way to get back on the team later."

"And you want to get back on."

"My dad thinks I can get a scholarship. Like Josh did. If Matusek gives me a chance to play and I show how good I am."

Somewhere there was a disconnect between what others thought of Anthony's ability and what he and his dad thought.

"It's not too late for that?" I said. "I don't know how the timing works."

"Josh's a year older than me. Ahead of me. So this year is when I need to shine."

"So you're a good player. Why do you think Coach Taylor cut you from the team?"

"He just hated some kids. For no reason. Started calling me names, telling me I sucked. So, yeah, surprise, I screw up. When someone yells at you all the time, you're not going to do good."

"I worked with some directors like that. I'm sure I did much worse in rehearsals because I thought too much about what I was doing. Made mistakes."

"Yeah, like that."

"But the team started winning. Do you think that was in spite of how Coach Taylor treated the team?"

"I guess, yeah. He was a better coach than the one before in a way. He knew more about basketball."

I drained the last of my malt. "So a good coach on how to play, terrible coach based on how he treated players?"

"Yeah."

That made some sense, though Anthony might simply be agreeing with me. "How long were you on the team last year?"

"Four weeks."

"What's Coach Matusek like?"

"Not as good as Taylor."

"I heard him call you a name that night. Are you worried he might be just like Coach Taylor?"

"He wasn't last year. But if I get to play, I can handle it if he is." His arms pressed to his sides, though, and he seemed to shrink lower in his chair.

"What does it mean? Drooler?"

"It's just a nickname." He sat straighter and his chin lifted.

"But it comes from somewhere."

"I dribbled the ball on my foot once, okay? And Coach Taylor, he said I wasn't dribbling I was drooling. That's the day he cut me from the team."

"And it doesn't bother you that Coach Matusek used it?"

"It's just a joke."

I remembered Rima saying Anthony got all red in the face when the other players said it. I couldn't imagine he felt better about a coach using it. But I didn't see a point in pushing him on it. He was already uncomfortable.

"Did Coach Matusek and Coach Taylor get along?"

"Oh, yeah. Matusek hung on his every word. Did everything he said. Started dressing like him. Some of the team kind of laughed about it. Like if Taylor decided to eat dog, uh, dog poop for lunch Matusek would ask for a double helping. They didn't say poop, though."

"I get it," I said, unsure what to make of Anthony seeing me as so much of a grown up that he couldn't swear in front of me. Nine or ten

years wasn't that much older than Kayla Mc-
Nulty, though maybe at sixteen I would have
thought so.

"Do you know Kayla McNulty?"

"New guidance counselor. Sweet." His entire
face flushed the color of his freckles and a shade
darker than his pumpkin-colored hair, so I
guessed sweet didn't just mean she was a nice
person.

"Is she your counselor?"

"I'm not that lucky. I got this old lady.
Wouldn't do anything to get me back on the
team."

"Is that something a guidance counselor
could do?"

"Well, Kayla's Josh's counselor, and he stayed
on the team."

"And you think that's connected?"

Based on what little I'd learned about Coach
Taylor, I couldn't imagine Kayla's input making a
difference.

"That's what my dad said. That maybe Kayla
convinced the coach because she's so – uh –
cute."

"Do you think your dad would talk to me?"

"What for?"

"About Coach Taylor, the team, how it all affected Josh. I'm assuming he knew Josh pretty well when you were friends."

He eyed me. "I mean, it's kind of weird. Are you, like some sort of spy for Josh's parents?"

Another worry about spying. Maybe the idea came up so much at this school because Coach Taylor worried about parents knowing too much about his coaching methods, and his paranoia filtered down to everyone else. Or it might have started at the top, with the principal. If that were the case, though, it seemed unlikely he would have so easily agreed to a stranger volunteering.

"I'm just what I said. A friend who's volunteering. And while I'm here, Josh's dad asked me to look out for Josh a little. See if I could figure out if there's anything he can do to help."

"It sounds like a spy."

"You can talk to Josh if you want to before you talk to your dad."

I'd just have to make a call to Beckwell and hope he could persuade Josh that it was all part of looking into the coach's death.

"I might." He looked at the table again, though, and I guessed he probably wouldn't. Whatever happened between the two boys, it hadn't ended well.

I fished out a business card and handed it to

him. Usually these days I just texted people my info, but I didn't want to text a student. "If your dad's willing to talk to me, he can call either number."

11

———————

SUMMER IS a wonderful time to live in Chicago, even for someone like me who doesn't love hot weather. I live less than two miles from Lake Michigan, so on most days it's about ten degrees cooler in my neighborhood than it is out in the suburbs. That meant when I met Lauren that night outside for dinner, rather than the sticky hot air in Riverside I got to feel a cool lake breeze.

Lauren's a real estate agent, and she had a condo showing in River North, a trendy neighborhood just west of downtown. I dropped the car off at home, not interested in paying thirty dollars to park for the evening. Plus, walking is my main exercise, so I walked the mile and a half to the section of Chicago's River Walk along

Wacker Drive. Down a flight of concrete steps are rows of restaurants and bars with outdoor seating along the river.

Lauren had gotten there before me and snagged a tall table along the river. Despite the crowds I spotted her easily. Her blond hair shone in the late evening sunlight, and her pink Dolce and Gabbana clutch purse sat on the table, its gold chain wound around her wrist, making clear she was a Chicagoan. Only the tourists and suburbanites let their purses hang freely on the backs of their chairs when dining outdoors. It's an invitation to pickpockets.

"Hope you wanted a whisky sour," she said. "Too hot for wine."

"Agreed."

I slid into the chair opposite Lauren and sipped the drink she'd ordered for me. The sharp lemon flavor and bit of pulp told me it was fresh lemon, and it was on the weak side, like mildly alcoholic fresh-squeezed lemonade. Perfect for me. I drink more for the taste than the alcohol.

"So? How's high school life?" Lauren said. "Seriously, spare no detail."

"As political as anywhere I've ever worked." I flipped over the laminated menu, looking for crab meat stuffed mushroom caps, my favorite at this restaurant. "Before the murder talk, there's something else. I've mentioned Eric to people because he plays basketball. But it's hard explaining how I know him. If I say my boyfriend's son, that's not right because Ty's my boyfriend. If I say my former boyfriend's son, that feels wrong because it's not like we broke up. Marco's dead. And then there's the word boyfriend. It doesn't really convey how serious Marco and I were, so I think it seems odd to people that Eric is still part of my life."

"Sure," Lauren said. "Also, you never call Ty your boyfriend."

I paused with my drink on the way to my lips. "Yes I do."

"Maybe in your head. But I've never heard you say it until now. And you've been seeing him, what, six months? All this awkwardness isn't about Marco, it's about Ty. Or it's about still seeing Marco as the most serious relationship in your life, not Ty."

"I haven't known Ty that long."

She raised her eyebrows and stared at me. Lauren and I have been friends since our first year of law school, though she quit, convinced law was not for her. Sometimes we don't need to say a word to be understood.

"Okay, right, I only knew Marco a few months," I said. "But that was different. We knew it was right so fast."

"Exactly. But you're keeping Ty at arm's length. Figuratively, anyway."

"He's getting over a long-term relationship, too. He's not in a rush."

"Quille, the guy is seriously smitten. He's holding off because he's not sure where you're at. Sooner or later he'll move on."

"No, that's – Okay. I'll think about that."

"Try not thinking so much. It might help."

The waiter brought our food as a speedboat veered to the edge of the concrete platform and docked. While people can't keep boats at this spot on the river, they can dock there temporarily while they eat dinner.

After the motor cut and we could hear ourselves again I told Lauren I was hoping she could help me understand the school atmosphere better.

Not only had she attended a Catholic high school, Lauren was active in her church, St. Peter's in downtown Chicago. She organized fundraisers and knew some of the priests well. Which meant she understood politics. I filled her in on everything I'd learned so far as we devoured mushroom caps and split a half pound burger with bleu cheese and bacon. No one ever said we ate healthy when we were together.

Lauren held up a finger. "Okay, first, sports and arts rivalry, totally a thing, at least at the high school I went to. Cheerleaders, football players, would not be caught dead trying out for a play. Stupid now that I look back on it. I would have made an awesome princess when my school did Once Upon a Mattress, don't you think?"

I laughed. "I do think. So you don't see it as odd that Polly suspects I'm there to help cut her department?"

"School like that? From what you told me, every department's worried about getting cut every day. Or they seriously should be. So maybe she's paranoid about it. People don't send their kids to Catholic school like they used to. And they don't have that many kids. My parents each had three siblings. But they only had me."

I shook my head. "But those are budget issues. I get that. But does she really think the school would send in an undercover volunteer to check her out? They must have oversight committees to look at finance."

"Huh. Yeah, they'd have admin people at least who go over the books. And I don't know why it would make her lock her door." Lauren stirred her drink, which was down to ice and a slice of lime.

The waiter stopped at our table and we ordered dessert. After he left, Lauren said, "Beckwell's wife is on the board?"

"Ex."

"Ask her. She'll know if there's some worry about embezzling that might relate to the theater department. Also if there's a petty theft problem. Might be why Polly's locking her door."

"Good idea."

When I told her more about the guidance counselor, Lauren thought the students calling Kayla by her first name sounded a little informal, but since they all seemed to do it she didn't find it odd that Josh did. "But it's seriously weird that she must have called or texted him right after the two of you met. Like, what, he's her BFF and they talk every night?"

"My thought exactly. Or he's her boyfriend."

"Ick. You know I like older guys, but a seventeen-year-old student with a faculty member?"

"Danielle's had a couple cases like that." My friend and officemate is a criminal defense attorney. "But I don't know that Josh'll tell me if I ask him outright, and I'm sure she won't. So I'm left with telling his parents and feeling bad if I'm wrong."

"Why else would they be so buddy-buddy? You seriously buy that there's something his parents won't listen to and this Kayla will?"

"If he doesn't want to play basketball anymore, and he thinks no one will let him off the hook, I can see where he might feel that way."

"Like you with theater," Lauren said.

"Right. Gram was the only one who wasn't disappointed in me."

"She's pretty practical. She was probably relieved."

"Maybe. But she also didn't say that. She gave me advice if I asked, but otherwise she left it up to me."

The waiter appeared with our dessert, a banana, caramel, and chocolate sundae to share. Lauren spooned extra caramel sauce on a banana, mashed it into the ice cream, and ate a few bites. I dug into the scoop of chocolate ice cream, which was topped with chocolate sauce and sprinkles.

"Say being on Josh's side means Kayla's the only one who stood up to the bully coach," Lauren said. "You can't assume he feels about basketball the way you felt about acting. Also, isn't Josh a suspect?"

"He's big enough," I said. "But no one reported him disappearing from the pep rally. Or looking disheveled or injured later."

"So no one on the team is a suspect?"

"They're not likely suspects. Maybe someone not on the team, though."

"Like Josh's friend Anthony. Could he have done it?"

"Physically? Taylor had a couple inches and at least forty pounds on him. Whoever did it had a weapon, but it was a knife. Not the same equalizer as a gun. You need to get close. So he'd have had to take the coach unaware."

"But a student could, couldn't he? A coach wouldn't expect a student to attack him. It could explain Josh knowing something and not wanting to say. If he knows his best friend killed the coach or suspects it. I'd never turn you in."

"I appreciate that. But the changes in Josh started months before the coach's death."

"Maybe Anthony was threatening the coach for a while before he confronted him."

"That goes against the taking him by surprise theory. But it supports the bully coach idea. Maybe Josh doesn't like basketball because

Coach Taylor was abusive." I watched a yellow kayak float by on the river, carried by the current as its inhabitant took a break from rowing. "Trouble is, if it's someone who didn't make the team or got cut that's a lot of suspects. Beckwell estimates at least twenty. I don't know how I'd narrow it down. Or rule out any of their parents for that matter."

Lauren ate the last of the ice cream. "Oh, definitely think about parents. They lose their minds about their kids and sports."

12

———

THE NEXT MORNING WALT DURKIN, Anthony's father, left me a voicemail while I was on a conference call with a client. I called him back and got his voicemail.

A little after noon, as I walked to Union Station to take the 12:30 to Riverside, my phone rang. It was him, so I answered, pressing my free hand to my open ear to block the sound of a jackhammer at a construction site off Ida B. Wells Drive. The six-lane street, which ends at one end at Michigan Avenue while the other becomes the Eisenhower Expressway, serves as an unofficial border between the neighborhood where I live and work and downtown Chicago.

"Anthony told you I'm a friend of Josh Beckwell's dad?" I said.

"Yes. He said you want to know about Coach Taylor. How he treated the players. Though I'm not sure I see the point. The man is gone. He can't retaliate against the students anymore."

Interesting that Walt didn't say "dead." The particular words people use hold a lot of meaning both in plays and legal arguments. But it might mean nothing in real life. Most people prefer euphemisms for death. I had grown up surrounded by it, including images of my deceased sister. I knew that no matter what you call it, you can't keep it at bay.

"Taylor retaliated against students if they complained about him?" I said.

"The students never complained. No one dared. But if they told their parents and the parents complained, he made life a living hell for the whole team. Then the team took it out on the kid."

"Did that happen to Anthony?"

"Of course not. I never complained."

I wondered if Anthony told him about the team members making fun of him and ostracizing him.

"Because you didn't have a problem with the coach?" I asked.

There was a long pause.

"Mr. Durkin?"

I had reached the Jackson Street entrance to the train station. The giant clock on a tower two blocks north told me I had eight minutes until my train left. Once I got inside there would be announcements and crowds, which would make it hard to hear. I stopped by the railing overlooking the river. The wind carried a mix of deep, rich chocolate from the factory a mile or so north and a faint, dank river smell.

"I wouldn't say Anthony didn't have a problem," Walt Durkin said. "Taylor treated the team members badly. Berated them. Called them names. But Anthony loves the game. Wants to play college ball. And he was dealing with all of it. Not that it helped."

"He got cut anyway. That must have been disappointing."

"Didn't matter." His voice was clipped. "He wasn't getting court time anyway. Not the way Taylor handled things."

"Is it different with Coach Matusek?"

"So far. Anthony might get back on the team. But you wanted to know about Josh."

I wondered if Walt really thought Coach Matusek treated students better or only wanted to believe it.

"I do." I glanced at the clock again. Time to get inside. "But I need to catch a train. Can we talk another time? In person?"

I always prefer to talk in person. Body language, tone of voice, and facial expressions reveal a lot.

"Not sure that's necessary," he said.

As I pushed through the glass doors and headed down the escalator, I told him about Josh's mood changes and his parents' worries. I could barely hear Walt, but he finally agreed to meet. I said I'd text him a few possible times and places and hung up.

Diesel fumes filled my lungs as I rushed along the platforms between trains. I made it on board a minute before the doors shut.

I had a lot of work to do, so I returned to my office that evening. When I felt caught up enough, I called Josh's mother. Nadine told me that since basketball season started Josh had little time for anything other than practice, so he rarely saw

Anthony or Walt once Anthony was off the team. So far as she knew, the friendship never resumed, despite that the boys had been close since third grade.

I asked about thefts at the school and told her how suspicious Polly seemed to be of me.

"No thefts I've heard about. And I don't know why she wouldn't want you there to help out," Nadine said. "Board members are always urging parents to volunteer, and the arts departments in particular need it. I thought she'd be thrilled."

She also told me Polly had no direct access to school funds. "If she were up to anything with the money, she'd need someone in accounting to help her. And the CPA who chairs our finance committee has an eagle eye. Hard to believe anything gets past her."

I spun my chair to gaze out my window, though my view is mainly of taller brick buildings a few blocks away, including the one I live in. I didn't want Kayla McNulty to lose her job if she hadn't done anything wrong, or to betray anything Josh might feel he told me in confidence. But boundaries matter in teacher/student relationships. And Josh's parents needed to know what might be going on with their son.

"Have you ever wondered if Josh might be too close with his guidance counselor?"

"Kayla? He talked with her a lot this year, but I encouraged it. That's what the staff is there for."

"When did he start talking to her?"

"Around the holidays. December."

"Is there any chance what's upsetting him is Kayla?"

"Are you telling me there's something going on?"

"Nothing I know of. She struck me as genuinely concerned about Josh. But the day after I talked to her, he confronted me, angry that I'd spoken to her. So she must have texted or called him the night before."

"That's against school policy." The pitch of Nadine's voice rose. "She can't text or call students other than for professional reasons."

"We don't know it wasn't for professional reasons," I said. As a lawyer, I've learned almost any fact can be used to prove more than one position. Only when I see everything together, and understand the ways opposite sides see things, do I feel like I get near the truth. "Josh called her a friend."

Nadine sighed, sounding a little like Beckwell for a moment. "When I was in high school, counselors, teachers, they weren't your friends. Now, everyone's supposed to be a buddy. Still, I need to talk to the principal. If she's preying on my son, it stops now."

"Did Josh say anything to you about Coach Taylor?"

"He said Taylor knew a lot about basketball. And made them work hard. But he hasn't exactly been talkative this year, so that's about it."

"Did he feel bad when Anthony got cut from the team? He got cut, by the way, he didn't quit."

"Really? I guess I'm not that surprised. Josh was thrilled when Anthony made the team, but he felt bad Anthony didn't get to play as often or get attention the way Josh did. Then once Coach Taylor took over, Anthony sat on the bench."

"When Anthony did play, what's your impression of his skills?"

"Average? I don't track statistics, but my husband does. He said Anthony was better off spending his time on something else."

Another way, in addition to both being police, that Wayne and her current husband were alike.

"You said before you never talked much with Anthony's dad. And Wayne's never met him. What about your husband?"

So far, Walt Durkin hadn't responded to my text proposing different meeting times, but maybe I could get some background info about him.

"No," Nadine said. "He tries to meet all Josh's friends. But he hardly ever meets the parents. He's second shift or night shift a lot. We don't socialize much with other couples."

"Have you seen Mr. Durkin at games? Does he argue with the coach?"

I was thinking of Lauren's comment about parents losing their minds over their kids and sports.

"Oh, sure, I've seen him at games. Never saw him argue. Or shout at his kid from the sidelines like some parents do. But he sits in the front row, and he concentrates so hard. Like he's memorizing every play. I told my husband I bet he goes over every second of the game with poor Anthony when he gets home."

After we ended the call, I sent a follow up text to Walt Durkin, then walked two blocks home to sit on my deck with a cool glass of water. The fresh scent from my neighbors' potted trees helped me relax. I let my mind drift rather than consciously sorting through what I'd learned. Sometimes that helped me put together arguments or sort through facts in a legal case.

Tonight, though, nothing seemed to lead anywhere. Especially my last conversation with Nadine, though I kept feeling she'd told me something key.

Yet what was there? There might or might not be something inappropriate between Kayla and Josh. That mattered for Josh's well-being, but I doubted it helped with Coach Taylor's murder. Not only was Kayla tiny compared to Coach Taylor, Beckwell had told me there was no question she was inside with four of her cheerleaders when he was killed.

Polly acted suspicious of me when I arrived, and she and Kayla both thought the coach bullied students. But nothing connected Polly to the coach's death. Former team members, kids who tried out and didn't make it, and their parents all might be angry at Coach Taylor. But I didn't have any way to contact all of them. The best I could do was get a feel for their overall mood by talking again to Anthony's dad. If I could convince him to meet me.

And Coach Matusek, the only person who obviously benefitted from Coach Taylor's death and who argued with Taylor the night before he died, had an alibi.

The lack of wind, unusual for my neighborhood, made it hot on the deck, but I wasn't ready to go in. I pressed the cool glass of water against the inside of my wrist, enjoying the icy slickness of it.

My mind kept returning to Polly. One of my strengths as an actor had been my ear for dialogue and my memory. If I pay attention closely, I can recall word-for-word what people say. It made it so much easier to memorize my lines for plays. It comes in handy as a lawyer, too, as I quickly recall what a witness said and when, making it easier to pull together threads and spot contradictions.

Now I replayed what Polly said about the argument she overheard. She guessed the man arguing with Coach Taylor was Matusek based on height, hair color, and the conversation. I shut my eyes and thought through my talk with Matusek at open gym. That's when it hit me. Not what Matusek said, but what I observed. When I first saw Anthony Durkin, not knowing who he was, I thought he might be the coach's son.

I hurried inside, pulled out my iPad, and

searched for photos online of St. Angelina basketball games. At last I found one that showed the crowd. I zoomed in on the front row. And there he was. He sat on the edge of the chair, elbows on his knees, chin jutting forward, mouth in a straight line, eyes staring straight ahead. Even in the chair, you could see his legs were longer than those of the people around him, and he sat nearly a head taller, even hunched forward. His hair shone red in the gymnasium lights.

Not surprisingly, Walt Durkin looked very much like his son. Who looked very much like Coach Matusek, the man Polly thought she had seen arguing with Coach Taylor not long before his death.

13

———————

"Based on an argument Walt Durkin might have had with the coach?" Beckwell said.

I was on my phone, squeezed into a tiny backstage corridor with make-up tables along a wall. It was a completely interior room that smelled of face paint. A door at one end led to the costume shop, the other to a hallway that led to stairs and a back entrance to the stage. I thought it would be perfect for my plan, which I had just outlined for Beckwell.

"Not just that," I said. "Walt Durkin was angry over his son being cut. It's all over his social media. For almost the entire year after that he complained about the coach. He also posted all kinds of photos of his son playing basketball, saying how great he was. After the coach's death there's nothing."

Walt had finally responded to my texts and we were meeting tomorrow after my rehearsal.

"Well, he had no reason to complain anymore," Beckwell said. "Taylor was dead."

"No, I mean nothing. No more photos of his son playing basketball, no more sports news. Nothing about St. Angelina's other than some reposts of other parents' positive comments about the school. It reads like a guy who absolutely doesn't want to draw attention to himself."

"None of which is enough to make him a suspect."

"Exactly. Which is why my plan. But it's likely to make Anthony madder at Josh whether I'm right or wrong. You're okay with that?"

"That I can deal with, and Josh will have to, too. Friendship's important, but Anthony's already cut Josh off. But I don't like it, Quille. A lot of things need to go right."

"I'll be careful."

"I've heard that before."

"Walt Durkin?" The principal rocked his chair forward and back. "He's our most reliable donor. Every fundraising letter, every benefit, every appeal, he comes through."

"Even after his son was off the team?"

"Even after. Shows real school spirit."

Wayne Beckwell had eased the way for me, calling the principal right after we hung up. Beckwell didn't tell Scott Galleti he'd asked me to come to St. Angelina's, but instead that I had started putting things together and talked with Wayne. Wayne assured him I had good instincts.

"That doesn't mean he didn't argue with the coach in the parking lot," I said. "It escalates, one of them has a knife, and Coach Taylor loses the battle."

"I can't accuse Walt – or anyone – without good reason."

"The good reason is what I'm aiming to get," I said. "Did Walt have access to the faculty parking lot that night?"

"Anyone could walk in. Even now, to tell the truth, it's only a matter of climbing the fence if you're on foot and in good shape. But you'd be recorded on security cameras."

"Which weren't there before."

"Right. Big mistake on our part, but there's

never been violence, beyond a few student fist fights, at St. Angelina's."

"Was Walt Durkin at the pep rally that night?"

"No. His son was off the team by then. Only parents of team members were invited. But he might well have picked Anthony up after the rally."

"And you're sure Anthony was there?"

"It was required for all the students. There were no absences. I remember because Coach Taylor was adamant about school support. Anthony, along with the other students, was inside the gym when Coach Taylor was killed."

"Okay, that's what I thought. Here's what I need from you. I'm meeting with Walt Durkin tomorrow night – "

Scott started shaking his head before I could finish. "No. No. I think you're wrong. But if you're not, I won't have you risking your life on my watch."

"But that's exactly what I'm thinking. On your watch."

Leaving out my second purpose for involving him, I explained my plan. It was guaranteed to keep him out of it entirely if I was wrong about

Walt. And, I hoped, to ensure my safety, though I felt less certain about that.

———

Walt Durkin had agreed to drive to the high school after work and meet me around six p.m. backstage. I told him I'd be there late finishing some tasks for the play next week.

Given the divide between sports and the arts at the school, I was banking on Walt not knowing his way around backstage. Before rehearsal that afternoon, I slipped into the costume shop, a small room with a couple old sewing machines and racks with decades of costumes and accessories that the theatre department mixed and matched for various productions. I shoved a rolling costume rack, one that had a metal shelf at the top, in front of a door in the middle of one of the long walls. The hanging costumes and the hat boxes on the shelf blocked the door from view.

It led to the long, narrow corridor the students used as a make-up room, the one I'd closed myself into for the call with Beckwell.

Scott Galleti arrived at quarter to six via that corridor so he could listen in. If I got Walt to reveal something incriminating, the principal's report along with mine should make him a suspect, allowing the police to take a DNA sample and fingerprints.

"I feel slightly ridiculous." Galleti perched on a stool in front of the make-up mirror. "Plus, once you shut that door, I won't be able to see."

"You don't need to see, just listen. But keep the door ajar, so you'll get some light. And be able to hear better. Just make sure you're quiet."

"What makes you think Walt Durkin will confess? If he's the one who did this."

"Walt's not a career criminal. Also, this isn't violence against a domestic partner. Most people who kill someone feel remorse. Guilt. They might not want to be caught or go to jail, but it's a hard thing to live with."

I had picked up a few things sharing an office with a criminal defense attorney and that was one of them.

I glanced at the time. "We need to test this out."

Scott Galleti shut the door nearly all the way and turned off the light. "The stolen cash and credit cards suggest a mugging."

I shifted the clothing rack into place, backed off several feet, then answered him at a normal volume. "The killer could have panicked and grabbed those to make it look like a mugging. The equivalent of a hit and run. And a personal conflict makes more sense with the rest of the facts. Can you hear me?"

"Loud and clear."

I rearranged some of the costumes and hangers to be sure they hid the door. "Your parking lots aren't visible from main roads. Only people who followed the high school's schedule would know anybody would be in the parking lot that night, so why wait there if it's a crime of opportunity? And the people who knew the parking lot would be used knew about the pep rally. Not the best time to plan a crime if you don't want witnesses."

I thought I heard a noise from the wider back stage area. I looked out the costume shop's main door, but there was no one.

Inside the shop again, I said, "You get all that?"

Scott's voice was muffled, but I could understand him. "Got it. You're saying instead of a mugger, more likely an angry parent waited there to confront the coach."

"Right. If he's not planning murder, there's no reason to worry about witnesses. That kind of person, especially one without any criminal history, killing someone is likely to weigh on his conscience."

"I don't know if I should hope you're right or you're not."

This time I did hear a door open and shut. I took a deep breath to calm my nerves, arranged what I thought of as my props, and crossed the room to open the main door to the back stage area.

14

———————

"Back here." I popped my head out the door and waved to Walt Durkin.

He wore khakis and a polo shirt and was a bit shorter and more broad shouldered than his son. After we introduced ourselves, I took my seat behind a battered wood table where I'd set out a sequined long-sleeved top and a threaded needle. Using small stitches, I added more sequins as we talked.

Walt half sat, half leaned against a closed Singer sewing machine that looked like one my Gram owned. "So what else do you want to know about Josh?"

"Before that, I need to tell you something. You seemed to think Coach Matusek might be treating the players better than Coach Taylor did. But my first night here I watched practice. Or I guess the 'right' term is open gym."

I didn't care about the wording at the moment, but if Walt found the language ridiculous, he might feel we were on the same page.

He nodded and smirked. "Gotta use the right term."

"Exactly." I set down the needle and thread, realizing it was white rather than yellow. Not the best color for sewing gold sequins. Hopefully Walt wouldn't notice. "He called your son Drooler."

"Matusek did?"

"In front of everyone. When Anthony lost control of the ball. I understand that's a nickname Coach Taylor started."

"Yeah, and it — I knew the students might keep saying it for a while. But not Coach Matusek."

"Anthony didn't tell you?"

Walt pinched the area above his nose with his forefinger and thumb. "Probably afraid I'd confront the coach."

"Would you?"

"No. Coaches have to be tough. Yelling,

calling a name once, sometimes they do it to motivate players."

"And Taylor did those kinds of things."

Walt nodded again. I wished he'd say it out loud for the benefit of Scott Galleti. It was why I chose him rather than Beckwell to watch my back. As principal, he needed to understand what these kids had gone through. Might still be going through.

But this wasn't a deposition where I could instruct the witness to answer verbally for the record.

"So you thought Taylor was just being a demanding coach, and that's why you didn't talk to anyone about it?" I said.

The old sewing machine creaked as Walt shifted position. "What's this got to do with Josh?"

"If Coach Taylor treated Josh badly, I'm thinking Josh might have been afraid to talk to his parents. If he wanted to stay on the team."

"That's my guess."

"But Anthony told you about it." I grasped the needle and thread and fumbled for a sequin. I wanted to keep working, as if the whole conversation had little weight. But I ought to have chosen an easier task. It was a struggle to keep my hands steady.

Fortunately, Walt was looking toward a stack of steamer trunks and old suitcases in the corner, remnants of a long ago production. "Because he knew I'd listen to him. And stay out of it."

"And you think Josh's parents wouldn't."

"Cop for a dad, cop for a stepdad? I don't see them standing for their kid being pushed around."

"Literally pushed?"

"Not physically. I would've stopped that."

I pulled the thread through, fastening another sequin to the shirt sleeve. "But there are other kinds of pushing. I was hoping you could tell me more about that."

"What good does it do?"

"If Coach Matusek thinks the way to win is to do what Coach Taylor did, isn't it worth trying to stop it?"

"He can't be as bad as Taylor."

I set down the needle and looked directly at Walt. "And if he is? Isn't it worth alerting the school about what happened before? For Josh? For Anthony?"

Walt's gaze dropped to the floor, as if studying

a crack that ran through three of the off-white tiles near his feet.

Something rustled behind me, possibly Scott Galleti moving, so I spoke again to cover the sound. "At least tell me what things Taylor did. Maybe I can talk to Josh, get him to open up about it. I know you've known him for a long time. It could help him."

He heaved a sigh, looked at the ceiling, clearly wanting to be anywhere but here.

"I already know there was name calling," I said. "And lots of criticism."

"He berated them," Walt said. "Whenever they made the smallest mistake. When they lost, when they didn't win by enough, if they got too cocky when they won. Told them they couldn't have friends who weren't on the team. Couldn't talk to kids who got cut."

I hoped that was enough for the principal to start listening to parents' concerns. If not, I guessed Wayne Beckwell and his ex-wife would be pressuring him.

"That's why Josh and Anthony stopped being friends?"

"That's what Anthony said. They used to play in the sandbox out in our back yard. Been friends that long." His voice faltered, and he cleared his throat. "Now I never see Josh."

"When did Anthony tell you what Coach Taylor was doing?" I said.

"The first thing was when Anthony's grandmother died last November. My mother. It was early in the season. Taylor got on Anthony for missing practice. To go to the wake for God's sake. I made Anthony come with, and I told the coach that. My mother lived with us. Helped raise Anthony."

"And Coach Taylor's response?"

"Benched him for the first two games. Threatened to cut him from the team."

"And he did cut him eventually. Was that why?"

"That alone? Maybe. All I know is my boy had a target on his back from then on. That's when Taylor started calling him names. It made him nervous. He did worse. That kind of pressure. It's terrible for a kid."

"More pressure than college ball would be?"

He had likely said enough already to persuade Scott Galleti to take the coaching issues seriously, but I wanted Walt to keep talking. Once you get a witness going on about one topic, they find it harder to clam up about other things. I hoped that would be true of Walt.

"He gets to college, it'll be worth it. But high school's about developing kids' talents. Not survival of the fittest."

"But not everyone can be on the team, right?"

"Why not? Small school. Everyone who wants to play should play."

Though he might not know it, the comment suggested Walt knew Anthony wasn't one of the best players. Otherwise, he would have protested that whether or not everyone should be on the team, Anthony certainly should be.

"And after that first incident, Anthony kept telling you what was happening?"

"He had to talk to someone. It helped him deal with it."

"Did you notice it having bad effects on him?"

"He was fine." Walt's lip trembled, though, and I suspected Anthony hadn't been fine at all.

"Josh hasn't been. He's not sleeping. He's losing weight. His grades have fallen."

Walt's back straightened. "I saw that. He still played well at the few games Anthony and I went to, but I could see the changes."

"And you tried to help Josh, didn't you? Because you cared about him."

"What? No. I cared, but I didn't – "

"One of the faculty heard you confront Taylor about how he treated Josh."

It was a guess on my part, but I felt sure Walt was the man Polly saw. And it made more sense that he was talking about Josh than about Anthony, who had been off the team for months by then.

"I – no, I didn't. I wouldn't."

"Was it Anthony you were talking about then? Because you were defending a team player. I was sure it was Josh. In the gym the night before the mugging. It's why I thought you'd be willing to tell me what was really going on, where the other parents are still afraid. But Taylor ignored what you said, told you he was the one running the team."

What I knew about the conversation, or seemed to know, must have convinced Walt it was pointless to keep denying it. "Oh. That. It was a conversation, not a confrontation."

"How did this conversation start?"

"I was at the school to meet with the fundraising committee. On my way out, I stopped by the gym and heard Taylor yelling at

Josh. I waited until practice ended and told him to lay off."

"Why did he yell at Josh?"

"Something about his footwork. Kid was near tears. Hated to see it."

Josh must have felt doubly terrible that his friend was off the team, he was on it, and his friend's dad stuck up for him.

"If you thought the way Taylor acted was damaging to Josh, you must have thought it damaged Anthony. Back when Anthony was on the team."

"I didn't. Not when Anthony told me. It sounded bad. But I thought that...it's no excuse for me not getting it. But a good coach pushes kids. Makes them work hard. And Anthony, he doesn't always push himself. He likes things easy."

"It sounds like you thought the coach might be tough, out of line sometimes, but not what qualified as bullying or abusive."

I had read a few articles in my research, and it seemed like a line a lot of coaches walked. And stepped over.

Walt squeezed his eyes shut. "Then I saw it for myself. With Josh. The coach was right in his face. Swearing, screaming, sweating. Looked like he might slug him any second. And Josh stood there, frozen. Taking it. The way he stood there, I knew. Knew it happened over and over. And over."

"Did you talk to Anthony about it?"

"When I got home. He tried to say the coach wasn't that bad. Because he still wanted to be on the team. To try again next year. And I thought, did I do that? Did I push him so hard to play ball that he was willing to go back to that man?"

"Did you believe Anthony? That it wasn't that bad?"

"I wanted to." But Walt's head moved from side to side, a slow shake that contradicted his words. "But all through the night all the things Anthony said when he was on the team came back to me. And the change in Josh. I never saw Josh scared before. Or shaking. Or dead silent. That's not Josh."

His voice had dropped almost to a whisper. He kept his right hand in his pocket. His left gripped the table behind him, as if he needed to hold himself in place.

"So you talked to Coach Taylor after the pep rally," I said. "Stood up for Josh. And Anthony. And all those kids."

"Someone had to say something. The kids

were afraid, the parents were afraid. All anyone cared about was winning."

Walt let go of the table and stood straight. His eyes lifted to meet mine. It made me uneasy. I gripped the needle and resisted the urge to glance over my shoulder at the costume rack hiding the doorway behind me. I knew Scott Galleti was barely ten feet away, though hidden.

"And you told the coach all of that?"

"All of it and more."

"And it got physical?"

"He shoved me. My back slammed against one of the cars. I dropped my laptop."

This fit the investigative reports Beckwell had been able to get his hands on. A parked SUV had scratch marks down one side that the owner said hadn't been there before. If the laptop was in a case with rivets or sharp corners, that could have caused the marks.

Walt took one step toward me, facing me, but his eyes looked beyond me. Seeing the scene from the past. "Brand new laptop. I heard it crack. And the guy laughed. At me. At my kid. Calling us wimps, weasels. I took a swing at him. Missed. He grabbed me by the throat."

One of Walt's hands rose to his neck. For much of the conversation, I had felt like I was leading him. But now I didn't know if I had control.

I stood. "Someone had a knife."

"Me." He eased his hand out of his pocket, as if he didn't want to alarm me.

I was alarmed.

A lot of my friends who work tech in theater carry an all-purpose tool that has knives, screwdrivers, and other attachments so they can fix things on the fly. Other people carry simple pocket knives. But Walt opened his hand to reveal a closed switch blade with a three-inch black handle inlaid with pearl.

I couldn't think of a use for a switchblade beyond scaring or stabbing someone.

"That's it. The knife you used?" I raised my voice, letting it waver so it sounded like I did it out of fear, not to alert anyone else. And, okay, it also wavered out of pure fear. "I'm not sure that's legal to carry. Especially in a school."

Illinois law is confusing on switchblades, and I felt certain Walt didn't care if he was committing a misdemeanor by possessing it. I backed away, and my shoulder blades brushed the hanging costumes.

"Probably not." Walt's eyes studied the knife as if he hadn't seen it before, and his thumb slid over the pearl inlay. "My grandfather left this to me. He was a tough guy. Not like me."

I'd been shifting from side to side, hoping I looked nervous, which I was, but moving a little more to my left each time. At last, I felt one of the vertical bars in the rack. I gripped it if steadying myself, still holding the needle in my right. "You used it to defend yourself?"

Walt moved to one side, too, so he was directly in front of me, the sewing machine no longer between us. "I'll show you."

Everything happened at once. Walt pressed a button on the black handle, and the blade shot out. Holding onto the vertical bar, I pushed off with my right foot, throwing all my weight backwards and to one side. It made the rack rotate, one side swinging forward into Walt as he lunged toward me. It was a move my best friend and I had done with empty racks as kids when we were offstage and bored, giving one another free spins. We'd gotten in trouble for it, but now I was profoundly grateful for doing it.

The rack, loaded with clothing, didn't spin like an empty one, but its impact threw Walt off balance. He grunted, shoes squeaking as he stumbled. The far side of the rack clunked against the back wall. More quick, short knocks as the hat boxes tumbled off the shelf. A man yelped. It came from my left and behind me, where I thought the door to the make-up corridor ought to be, though I'd become disoriented with the spinning.

I scrambled in that direction, but became tangled in a long, lightweight coat. Breathing hard, tasting the fabric in my mouth, I poked the needle out as Walt lumbered toward me. Limited by the coat, I couldn't aim very well but I twisted my whole body and managed to scrape the side of his forearm. My nose banged some part of the rack and I yelled right along with Walt. The pain shot to my head, making me dizzy. I dropped the needle and put my hands out, hitting the wall.

As I steadied myself, I heard scuffling and blows landing behind me, then clatter as what must be the knife hit the tile floor. I finally freed myself from the coat. I spun and gripped the costume rack again, the other hand against the wall as Galleti slugged Walt. Despite being the larger of the two men, Walt stumbled backwards and to one side, moving a couple steps toward me.

Anchoring myself between the wall and the rack, my face sticky with blood from my nose, I kicked as hard as I could. My foot connected stomach flesh. Walt let out a whoosh of air, bent over, and fell to the floor, curled in a ball, gasping.

The knife lay a foot from Walt, but Scott Galleti grabbed it. A thin trail of blood ran down the side of the principal's face.

A maintenance engineer who had heard the noises barreled in. He and Galleti sat on Walt to keep him down while I found my phone and called the police.

15

"I HEARD MOST OF IT," Scott Galleti said. "Started inching out before you said that about the knife, but I was trying to keep him from hearing me. Didn't count on those hat boxes raining down on me."

We sat in his office after the police left. Scott had found a teabag in the administration's kitchen area and made me a hot cup of tea, insisting I needed something to calm down. His jawline was bruised and the edge of one of the boxes had sliced a cut not much deeper than a paper cut on his forehead. I, on the other hand, ached all over and had bruises on my arm, which must have hit the clothing rack at some point, and a very swollen nose.

"We tested the sound, but not the blocking." When he looked blank, I added, "Blocking is staging. Where actors stand and move on stage."

"I'll take your word for it. But it worked out. I got the impression the police will deal with Walt Durkin."

"And you'll look at Coach Matusek?"

"That was the main reason you led Walt to talk about the coaching issues, wasn't it? So I'd wake up to how Taylor and now Matusek treated the players?"

"It was a big part of it. Though it doesn't hurt for the prosecutor to have testimony that Walt had a motive. Assuming the DNA matches and he's the one who killed Taylor."

"You still think it might not have been him? Why would he lie?"

"To protect his son," I said.

Forensics, though, showed Walt Durkin's DNA on Coach Taylor's body. He'd left partial fingerprints on Taylor's wallet when he emptied it. The carelessness suggested that he might be telling the truth about not having planned an attack. But I didn't quite buy his claim of self-defense, and I wasn't sure a jury would. And he certainly wouldn't have an easy time avoiding what he'd just done to Scott Galleti and me. Beckwell also told me that a neighbor had gone swimming at a health club the next day with Walt and never noticed any bruising on his neck or torso.

Scott Galleti kept his word and interviewed Coach Matusek and the students. Matusek agreed to alter his coaching style, stop the required open gyms, and allow parents to attend practices. I wanted to believe he truly preferred a kinder coaching style, but he might just not want to end up like Coach Taylor.

The athletic department didn't plan to allow all kids who wanted to join to be on the team or all players to have equal playing time. But Matusek agreed to work in more playing time for each player. Tryouts would be held anew in the fall.

Josh finally told his parents about the abuse from Coach Taylor, and in my view it was abuse. The coach had never hit the students, but he belittled and berated them constantly, whether they did well or poorly. Josh came to hate being on the team. Only the fact that he had the scholarship kept him playing. He said he hoped next year he'd enjoy it. If not, he was reconsidering playing college ball. Something I could tell didn't thrill Detective Sergeant Beckwell, but he told me it was more important that his son be healthy and happy than that he get a free ride in college.

"Though it looks like I might never retire," he said. "Another tuition bill. Right when my oldest is finally done."

I shut my laptop and clicked off my office desk lamp. "You're a good dad."

My parents had never suggested sharing my college expenses with me. My dad left his full-time job when I was sixteen, and he and my mom moved back to Southern Illinois to be nearer to my sister's grave, leaving me with Gram. Seeing Beckwell take it for granted that he needed to do this for his son made me slightly envious. I hoped Josh appreciated having a dad who put him first.

On the other hand, Beckwell clearly loved his job. I didn't see him retiring any time soon no matter what.

"And Kayla McNulty?" I grabbed my shoulder bag off the credenza.

"Worked it out. Nadine and her husband and I talked with Josh and met with her and the principal. Kayla and Josh agreed she'd been encouraging Josh to tell us about the coach's behavior.

She said she tried to be more like a friend to all the students in the hope that they'd feel freer to talk to her."

As I stepped into the reception area, my officemate walked in, just back from visiting a client in jail. We waved at each other.

"And you believe her?" I said to Beckwell.

"I do. But going forward, she knows she needs to stick to the rules on texting and phone calls. Finally something everyone agrees on in my family."

"Including Josh?" I said.

"He's upset that we're treating him like a baby we have to watch out for. His words. But he'll get over it. He and Anthony started mending fences."

I reached the elevator banks but didn't push the button yet. I wanted to finish the call first. "Tough for Anthony these days."

"Yep. His dad's out on bond. Josh says Anthony and his mom are in shock."

"They had no idea?"

"Hard to say. The wife confided in my ex. Said Walt had a bad temper, yelled a lot, but was never physically violent. Maybe the coach did threaten him, and he just lost it. Or he meant to threaten the coach, scare him, and things got out of hand."

A few weeks later I heard from Beckwell. He wanted to meet on a Wednesday night.

This time I chose the spot, inviting him to Sociale, a small plates restaurant and bar in my neighborhood. It's on a corner, and two of the walls open all the way when the weather is warm, creating an indoor-outdoor sort of space.

Lauren joined us. Beckwell had offered to buy as a thank you and said I could bring a friend.

"So you seriously owe Quille now, don't you?" Lauren said after the waiter uncorked a bottle of Tempranillo and poured two glasses. Beckwell had asked for beer and seemed nonplussed at the long list of craft beers and ale.

"I do." Beckwell lifted his glass in a toast. "And not just for helping get a killer behind bars."

"Helping?" Lauren said. "You think the Riverside police were ever going to catch Walt?"

Beckwell sipped his Goose Island Brewery pale ale. "Not bad. And to answer your question, no comment."

"That," Lauren said, "is not an answer."

"And Josh? Is he doing better?"

"Seems happier. I really appreciate it, and I have something for you. But first, remember your questions about Polly?"

I nodded. "Does she have some connection to the murder?"

"None. But she is a cousin of the new comptroller. Polly recommended him, and Principal Galleti didn't think anything of it. But it looks like in all the confusion over Taylor's death and various requisition orders, the cousin managed to divert some funds."

"Polly was involved?"

"From what I hear, it looks like she caught on and didn't report it. Either to get a cut or out of loyalty. She may have been locking her office because she had some sort of proof there. And it's most likely why she was suspicious of you."

I dipped a piece of bread in fragrant olive oil with basil and fresh garlic. "I hope she wasn't. Involved. I liked working with her. And the kids."

"So it was a good thing volunteering," Beckwell said.

"It was."

"Still a seriously large amount of time away from her law practice." Lauren's gold bangle bracelets jangled as she pointed at Beckwell.

"That's why not only will I owe Quille a favor, I have a gift."

He slid an envelope across the table.

"Looks too thin to have a stack of hundreds in it," I said.

"Funny. Open it."

Inside was a certificate for a private course with a man whose name I didn't recognize.

"Needing some backstory," I said.

"Retired police academy instructor. Excellent for those who want to learn basic fighting, self-defense, and weapons training."

"Do I want to learn that?"

"Oh, you totally do," Lauren said. "Quille learning combat. I love it."

Beckwell frowned. "Not combat. This is about staying safe, de-escalating situations, avoiding danger, and fighting as a last resort. A very last resort." He started to shake his finger at me, then let his hand drop on the table. "You're still going to be smaller and slimmer than most opponents you might face. And you'll still be less used to violence than the average mugger and more apt to freeze. So this is not encouragement to engage in more risk taking than you already do."

"You're filling me with confidence." I put the envelope in my shoulder bag.

"I hope I'm filling you with caution. But you keep getting into these types of investigations, this time with my encouragement. Obviously you're not stopping any time soon. So I want to give you the best possible chance to protect yourself."

"I understand what you're saying. Believe me, I'll take advantage of it. If I don't, my friends will hound me."

"I will, too. Call first thing tomorrow," Beckwell said.

I smiled. "Is email okay?"

"He's sixty-eight, Quille. Likes to actually talk to people. Call him on the phone."

"Just giving you a hard time, Mr. Observant," I said. "There's no email listed here."

"You'll call?" Beckwell said.

"I'll call."

"Glad that's settled." Lauren waved toward the street. "Look who's finally here."

I twisted around to look. Ty threaded his way through the planters, still dressed for work in a suit with narrow-legged pants, and a collared shirt open at the neck.

"I'm buying for someone else?" Beckwell said.

"You don't have to buy for him," I said. "But I wanted you to meet my boyfriend."

ABOUT THE AUTHOR

In addition to the Q.C. Davis Mystery series, which includes *The Worried Man*, *The Charming Man*, *The Fractured Man*, and *The Troubled Man*, Lisa M. Lilly is the author of the *Awakening* supernatural thriller series and the host of the podcast *Buffy and the Art of Story*.

Her stories and poems also have appeared in numerous publications.

A resident of Chicago, Lilly is an attorney and a past Vice President of the Alliance Against Intoxicated Motorists. She joined AAIM after an intoxicated driver caused the deaths of her parents in 2007. Her book of essays, *Standing in Traffic*, is available on AAIM's website.

You can read the first three Q.C. Davis Mysteries in the box set/omnibus edition.

ALSO BY LISA M. LILLY

Q.C. Davis Mystery Series

The Worried Man (Q.C. Davis 1)

The Charming Man (Q.C. Davis 2)

The Fractured Man (Q.C. Davis 3)

The Troubled Man (Q.C. Davis 4)

Q.C. Davis Mysteries 1-3 Box Set/Omnibus

No Good Deeds (Short Story for e-newsletter subscribers)

No New Beginnings (Short Story for e-newsletter subscribers)

The Awakening Supernatural Thriller Series

The Awakening (Book 1)

The Unbelievers (Book 2)

The Conflagration (Book 3)

The Illumination (Book 4)

The Awakening Series Complete Supernatural
Thriller Series Box Set/Omnibus

Other Fiction

When Darkness Falls (a standalone supernatural
suspense novel)

The Tower Formerly Known As Sears And Two Other
Tales Of Urban Horror